DAVENPORT HOUSE 4

—HEIRESS INTERRUPTED—

DAVENPORT HOUSE 4

HEIRESS INTERRUPTED

MARIE SILK

Cover art by SelfPubBookCovers.com/Fantasyart

ISBN: 978-09973352-8-6 (print)
ISBN: 978-09973352-2-4 (ebook)

Marie Silk Publishing
P.O. Box 873
Hayden ID 83835

mariesilkpublishing@gmail.com

Davenport House Books by Marie Silk

BOOK ONE
Davenport House

BOOK TWO
Davenport House
A New Chapter

BOOK THREE
Davenport House
A Mother's Love

BOOK FOUR
Davenport House
Heiress Interrupted

BOOK FIVE
Davenport House
For the Cause

Chapter 1

"Nellie, try this one." Mrs. Whitmore handed her daughter another hat with seemingly endless frills.

"Mother, this is outrageous," Nellie replied, pulling at the excess of feathers and buttons.

"It is the only way you will have the biggest hat in the parade," her mother answered.

Nellie rolled her eyes. The Easter Parade in New York City was an important event to most upper class families, but not to her. She would rather be doing anything than parading down the street in a hat that weighed as much as a lap dog.

"I do not care if it is the biggest. I cannot wear this silly thing," Nellie argued, much to the dismay of the store clerk. The clerk gingerly lifted the hat from Nellie's grasp and placed it back among the display shelves.

"You need to be noticed if you are to catch a husband," Mrs. Whitmore reminded her. "You are not getting any younger. You must be noticed now, before it is too late."

"Why would it be too late?" Nellie asked curiously. Her mother was about to answer just as Mr. Whitmore emerged through the door of the hat shop.

"Haven't you ladies decided yet?" he huffed, looking

over the dozen hats displayed near his daughter. Nellie shook her head and Mrs. Whitmore gave her husband a look. Mr. Whitmore turned to the clerk. "We will take all of them," he muttered, eager to bring the shopping trip to an end. Nellie shook her head, knowing that she already owned more hats than she would ever wear. The clerk scurried away happily to collect enough hat boxes. Mr. Whitmore gave his wife a look that seemed to ask a question, but she shook her head in response.

"What is it?" Nellie asked.

"We will explain later, when we get back to the house," her mother answered.

The Easter Parade was in full swing the next afternoon. Ladies strutted through the street as expected with their showy hats and dresses. Some held ornate parasols and the spectators oohed and awed. Nellie shook her head as she pinned on the hat covered in flowers and other notions that her mother had finally chosen. She sighed at her reflection in the vanity mirror. "This is hideous," she grimaced. "At least Mother will be happy." Nellie joined the other ladies walking down the street and smiled at the people watching, who were busy judging among themselves who was the best dressed. Nellie could not help but laugh at the absurdity of it all. She wondered if her friend Mary would believe how silly everyone got about the Easter Parade. Mary Davenport lived in the countryside of Pennsylvania and did not often leave home for such events.

When the parade was finally over, Nellie stretched her neck in relief, removing the heavy hat from her head. "Nellie!" her mother scolded. "We are not even back to the hotel yet." Ladies were not considered fully dressed in public without their hats.

Nellie groaned. "Can't I go sit in the carriage until Father is through talking with those men?"

"Wait a moment, there is someone I would like you to meet first. He is son to the Goldsteins, and he has expressed an interest in getting to know you," Mrs. Whitmore said with a smile.

"Which one is he?" Nellie asked. Mrs. Whitmore discreetly nodded her head in the direction of a man who was approaching them. When Nellie saw the man, she made a face at her mother, at which Mrs. Whitmore returned a stern look.

"Mr. Goldstein, allow me to introduce my daughter, Nellie," Mrs. Whitmore greeted.

Simon Goldstein smiled wide at the attractive young lady in front of him. Nellie had a fair complexion framed in delicate blonde curls. She never had trouble gaining the attention of men, she simply did not care for the ones she met. "I am pleased to make your acquaintance, Miss Whitmore," Simon told her.

Nellie forced a smile. "I am pleased to make your acquaintance," she replied quietly.

"Your hat is—elegant," he stammered.

Nellie could not help but laugh. Another stern look from her mother caused Nellie to turn to Simon and speak quickly. "Thank you. I was just leaving to wait in my father's carriage. I must get out of the sun. Good day, Mr. Goldstein." Nellie turned on her heel and left the sidewalk.

"Forgive me, Mr. Goldstein. My daughter seems weary from the days' events. Please visit us in Lancaster sometime when you have the chance," Mrs. Whitmore apologized. Simon nodded and went on his way. Mrs. Whitmore arrived at the carriage where her daughter was waiting.

"What was wrong with Mr. Goldstein?" she asked, sounding tired.

Nellie shrugged. "He does not have the sort of face I like," she answered, even though she did not have a good reason for disliking him.

"Well, what sort of face *do* you like?" Mrs. Whitmore pleaded.

Nellie smiled dreamily. "You have seen the stable boy at Davenport House. I like his face very much."

"You know that such an arrangement is terribly improper, and do not say this to your father. You know how it provokes him to hear you talk of the Davenport's stable boy. Your father has not worked this hard to secure our future to see it all go to a servant who lives with horses." Mrs. Whitmore looked exasperated of having this conversation with her daughter. She leaned back against the leather seat and closed her eyes, waiting for the carriage to take them home to Lancaster.

It was weeks later while at their grand house that Mr. Whitmore summoned his daughter to the drawing room. He stood by the marble fireplace, leaning his elbow on the mantle with one arm while he held his pipe with the other. Nellie came to the room obediently and saw her mother reclined on a fainting couch. Mrs. Whitmore smiled when Nellie entered the room and Nellie smiled back. "What is this about?" she inquired.

"You should sit down for this," Mr. Whitmore suggested. Nellie seated herself next to her mother, who appeared unusually pale and wore a shawl around her shoulders.

"Are you feeling ill, Mother?" Nellie asked in concern.

"I am with child, Nellie," Mrs. Whitmore answered softly.

Nellie raised her eyebrows in surprise. "Oh, Mother, how wonderful! I adore babies."

"This changes things for you, Nellie," her father continued in a business-like manner. "It is a family tradition for the eldest male to inherit entirely. Your mother and I have chosen to keep this tradition, if we indeed have a son."

"Do you mean to say that I will inherit nothing if the baby is a boy?" questioned Nellie.

"You understand correctly. However, if we are to have another daughter, the fortune will be divided between the two of you equally," her father answered.

Nellie stared in bewilderment. She had never considered that she could lose her inheritance. It was a certainty that she had taken for granted her whole life. "But, how will I live?" Nellie asked.

"This is why we we wish to send you to London," replied her father. "We hope to see you make a favorable match for which we will even supply a dowry. It is not the way that I would prefer it, but you insist that you are unable to find a husband in America. Your Aunt Lucinda has already lined up potential suitors who are sure to meet with my approval."

"You never approve of *my* choices," Nellie pouted.

Mr. Whitmore rolled his eyes. "If this is about that stable boy again, I will not hear another word of it. I do not even want you associating with the Davenports. That family is in the midst of a loathsome scandal."

"But Mary is my dearest friend," Nellie protested. "She had nothing to do with the dreadful actions of her family."

"That family cost us five hundred dollars this year. My decision is final. Do not be so gloomy, Nellie. You will soon be sailing on the Lusitania and meeting new friends of desirable standing."

"But Mother should not take such a journey in her condition," Nellie commented.

"Your mother is not going. We are sending you with the Caswells as your chaperons," her father explained.

Nellie wrinkled her nose. "The Caswells are terribly boring. Can't I travel with someone more fun?"

"Do not even think of asking Mary Davenport," her father said sternly, seeming to know what Nellie was thinking.

"Mary is in mourning for her father," Nellie reminded him. "But perhaps I might take another friend with me."

"So long as it is a well-behaved young lady whose family is not in the midst of scandal," Mr. Whitmore muttered. "I will arrange for it. Do not forget to keep your mother's condition a secret until your marriage is settled."

Nellie went back to her room and thought about who she could ask to accompany her. Many of the ladies Nellie's age were either married and occupied with their wifely duties, or engaged and planning their weddings. Nellie was twenty years old and did not feel prepared to settle down into a stuffy house with a husband who could order her around. She sometimes thought that she would never marry at all, since she did not have the need before. Now that her inheritance was threatened, she realized she would have to begin thinking differently. She kept thinking of her friend Mary and how it had been too long since she had seen her last.

"Gladys," Nellie addressed her maid. "Order the car for me. I wish to visit a friend."

Nellie Whitmore arrived at Davenport House that day. She went to the sitting room with Mary and Abigail, who was Mary's companion. Nellie was surprised to also see Clara with them in the sitting room, yet socializing without her usual maid's uniform. That was when Mary explained to Nellie that Clara was recently discovered to be her half-sister. Clara was the daughter of the housekeeper and Mary's father, who was Master of the house. After the death of their father, Mary recognized Clara by relieving her of maid duties and allowing her to move upstairs as a member of the family.

Nellie's eyes were wide as Mary relayed the details of this lesser known scandal of the Davenport family. Nellie would not mention such a thing to her father, who was already against her associating with them. She looked back and forth between the sisters. "Well! Who would have guessed it? You two don't look a thing alike," she laughed. "You are lucky. My family does not have any interesting secrets at all!" She decided not to mention that she was on the verge of losing her inheritance because of a new heir. She was grateful for this distraction from the things happening in her life. Nellie turned to her new friend. "Oh, poor Clara, you have had no proper debutante. I will make introductions for you. You must learn how to navigate society and you must do it quickly," she said with a twinkle in her eye.

Clara seemed elated. "Would you truly introduce me?"

"Of course! It would be such fun! Oh dear, it may have to wait though. I have nearly forgotten that I am sailing for Liverpool in just over a week! I must think up a plan. In the meantime, let us take a walk to the stable—to see the horses of course."

They walked together toward the pasture where Nellie immediately spotted the handsome stable boy. "Good afternoon, Ladies," Ethan greeted. "Will you be wanting to ride today?"

"Oh, we are just taking a walk. Won't you come with us?" coaxed Nellie. "It seems so long since I saw you last, Ethan. How have you been?"

"Fine thank you, Miss Whitmore," he replied as he joined the girls. They walked the perimeter around the fence and watched the horses graze in the pasture. Nellie talked with Mary about how empty her stable was, now that she had a motor car.

"William said that he will buy an automobile next week for his medical practice," Mary told her.

"Oh yes, your new doctor. Have you fainted again while he is nearby, Mary?" Nellie teased. Mary turned red and looked away, confirming Nellie's suspicion that Mary thought of him as more than a doctor or a friend.

The conversation turned to horseback riding as they continued to watch the horses. When Clara admitted that she had never learned to ride, Nellie became excited about the things that she would introduce her new friend to. "There is much to see, Clara. I cannot wait to show you," she chatted, feeling an idea come into her head. "Oh, I have just realized a perfect solution! You must come to New York and take the voyage to Liverpool with me! I will introduce you to London society, who will not have heard a thing about your past. You may even fall in love with a man of title there. They are wild about rich American girls. I can hardly keep them away. It is a splendid idea, you must come!"

Clara was beaming. She had been wanting the chance to see the world away from Davenport House for years. Mary also seemed pleased for her. "What a grand opportunity for you leave and meet new people, Clara," she remarked in awe. "What do you think?"

"Nothing would make me happier!" Clara exclaimed. "But, did you not say that you are leaving next week? Do we have enough time to arrange it?"

"Oh, I will handle that, don't you worry. I will just telephone them to change my reservation. Honestly Mary, you are living in the Dark Ages out here with no automobile or telephone. Clara, you will love the Lusitania. It is gorgeous! The dining room is like a palace," Nellie continued on about the beautiful ship.

Clara could hardly contain her excitement. "I will need new dresses! Oh, I cannot believe it!"

Nellie's mind was bursting with ideas. "We will arrive in New York a day early so we can buy whatever you need there. If you like modern, you will fall in love with New York."

"I cannot wait," grinned Clara, her heart nearly beating out of her chest.

Later that evening when Nellie returned home, she explained to her father that she had found a traveling companion for the voyage. She left out the fact that Clara was now a Davenport.

"What is her name?" asked Mr. Whitmore skeptically.

"Clara Price," answered Nellie. It was not completely a lie, since Clara's surname had always been Price when she was a housemaid.

"Price...Price..." her father mumbled, furrowing his brow as he tried to think which family the girl must belong to. He shot a look at Mrs. Whitmore, who shrugged her shoulders.

"And how do you know this girl?" asked Mr. Whitmore.

"She is an acquaintance of Mary," Nellie answered quietly.

"Is she a well-behaved sort of girl?"

"Of course she is!" Nellie answered, feigning offense that her father would question it.

"Very well, we will arrange for her to accompany you. So long as it is agreeable to her parents," Mr. Whitmore added. "And I would like to meet this girl."

"I will inform her," Nellie replied. She then bounced up the staircase in excitement, thinking that this voyage with the Caswells might not be so boring after all.

She collected the advertisements from her parents that showcased the inside of the ship. There were luxurious suites for the first-class passengers, as well as a grand dining room serving ten-course meals. Nellie gazed at the pictures dreamily and wondered what sort of men her Aunt Lucy had lined up for her in London—and more specifically, if any of them were handsome.

The following week, Nellie went to Davenport House to meet with Clara about the upcoming voyage. Nellie and Clara were in the upstairs sitting room with Mary and Abigail. But Clara did not seem as enthusiastic about Nellie's visit as she had the last time. Nellie passed around the pictures of the ship to the girls while she chatted about the Broadway play they would be seeing in New York the night before they left.

Clara suddenly spoke up. "Nellie, I am terribly sorry, but I am afraid that I will not be able to accompany you after all."

Nellie's mouth hung open in surprise. "I do not understand. Has something happened?" she asked.

"My mother will not allow me to go. She has been sick

with worry ever since I mentioned the voyage, and I do not wish for her to be tormented any further," Clara explained.

Nellie did not try to hide her disappointment. "This is dreadful," she said with a pout. "I have already sent a telegram to Aunt Lucinda about my bringing a companion. I was looking forward to having the company. Oh, I do not want to spend six whole days alone."

Clara seemed to have a reply before Nellie had even reacted. "I did think of a solution just last night," Clara told her confidently. "Abigail may accompany you in my place. She would make a marvelous companion for you, and she has never been outside of Pennsylvania."

There was an awkward moment where no one spoke. Nellie was happy to take Clara to London with her as a favor to Mary, but did not dream of stealing Mary's companion away for the voyage. Nellie was aware that Mary loved Abigail and often spoke of how she could not do without her. She wondered if Abigail and Mary had already spoken of this arrangement before Nellie arrived. Otherwise, she could not think why Clara would suggest such a thing. "Well, I would be happy to have you, dear Abigail, but only if Mary can spare you," Nellie replied.

Mary seemed hesitant. "I will be quite busy with the estate while the new stable is being constructed. Abigail is free to go with you…if she wishes."

Nellie looked at Abigail, who finally answered in her usual meek way. "I am honored that you would consider taking me with you, Nellie. I will go, if it is what you and Mary wish."

"How wonderful," Nellie responded with a smile, feeling a renewed sense of spirit in knowing the voyage would not be so lonesome. "I will make the necessary arrangements. My father has expressed a wish to meet you before the journey. I hope you don't mind. Tomorrow, I will bring you to visit us in Lancaster. Oh, don't worry— my father is not as cross as he looks. He will be glad to meet you. I am sure of it."

The next day, Nellie brought Abigail into the grand drawing room of the Whitmore mansion where Nellie's parents waited to receive her. Abigail had been to the mansion once before, but was again impressed by the costly accents and furnishings. It was a room fit for royalty.

"Mother, Father, this is my friend Abigail," Nellie declared.

Mr. Whitmore looked Abigail up and down, but his skeptical stance relaxed slightly and he again rested his elbow on the fireplace mantle. "I thought you said her name was Clara Price," he replied gruffly. Mrs. Whitmore, who was reclined on a chaise lounge nearby, looked toward Abigail with an apologetic smile.

"I forgot to tell you that Clara's mother cannot spare her after all. Abigail has kindly agreed to accompany me instead," Nellie explained.

Mr. Whitmore raised an eyebrow but continued to glance in approval toward Abigail. "At least you look like the sort of girl who will keep my Nellie out of trouble," he muttered. "And your parents are agreeable to this voyage?"

Abigail cleared her throat before she answered. "My mother has passed on, Mr. Whitmore, and I have been away from my father's house for several years now."

"Very well," Mr. Whitmore agreed. He suddenly changed his tone to one of optimism. "I am grateful to you, Abigail, and I will telephone Cunard about the change. I am now satisfied that Nellie has reconsidered the value of this voyage. She will have no reason to be in sore spirits about it now that she has you."

Nellie took Abigail to her bedroom after the meeting with her parents. "My father seems to like you, and he doesn't much like anyone," Nellie commented. "He hardly likes me. Do you want to know a secret?"

Abigail nodded shyly in response.

"My mother is expecting," Nellie continued. "Father said that if the baby is a boy, I will lose my inheritance altogether! He does not care if I am left destitute, so long as he has a son. That is the true reason I am being sent to Aunt Lucy in London."

"I see," Abigail replied. "I am sorry, Nellie. That must have been difficult news for you to hear."

Nellie sighed thoughtfully. "I will be happy to have a brother or sister, but it does not make me comfortable to conceal such a fact when I am meeting suitors. They are likely only expressing interest because of my family's money anyway. Mother and Father intend for me to marry before the suitor can find out that I may have none."

"It does seem dishonest," Abigail frowned.

"Do you think that I should tell the truth? I may become rather unpopular in London once word spreads."

"But how much better would it be to begin your marriage with a lie?" Abigail asked gently. "What will happen with your inheritance if your mother's baby is a girl?"

"I will inherit half the estate. Father said that I would also keep the house as the firstborn daughter, but it is still less than a suitor might expect of me. Father did say he will provide a dowry for when I go to Britain."

"Yes, I suppose the English do insist on a dowry," Abigail remarked, wrinkling her nose.

"You sound as if you don't like the English," Nellie laughed.

Abigail giggled. "I imagine there are many English who are just the same as everyone else. But they did give our blessed Ireland a terrible time. I try not to have bad feelings for them, but I was raised with unfavorable talk of the English all my life."

Nellie giggled. "You will be seeing many English soon. Mary is only half-English, you know. Her mother is Irish."

"Mrs. Davenport?" asked Abigail in surprise. "She seems to be very hard on everyone, no matter their origins. I would not have guessed that she came from the same place as my family."

Nellie shrugged. "She has been difficult as long as I've known Mary. I don't understand it either. Can you believe that Mary's father had a child with the housekeeper?"

Abigail could feel her cheeks turning red. She did not feel comfortable talking about Mary or her family behind their backs. "It was a surprise—but Mary speaks of her father endearingly. I believe he must have been a good man."

"Oh, of course he was. I did not mean to suggest that he wasn't," Nellie added. "You are entirely too kind, Abigail. I see now why Mary loves you so much."

"Thank you," Abigail replied. "It is kind of you to consider me for your voyage to London. I am nervous, but you seem a wonderful lady to travel with. I can see why Mary loves you, too."

The next day, Nellie went to Davenport House to retrieve Abigail for the journey. When they arrived in New York, they checked into The Grand Hotel on Broadway, where they would meet the Caswells. They were the husband and wife who agreed to chaperon Nellie. As the bellhop showed Abigail to the suite, she whispered to Nellie, "I never thought that I would stay in a hotel as a guest. I used to be a hotel maid, although it was not in a hotel as grand as this one. I am grateful to you, Nellie."

"It is my pleasure," Nellie replied. "Let us change our clothes. We must meet my chaperons for dinner. They are terribly boring, but we need not see them much once we are on the ship."

They went into the hotel dining room to find Mr. and Mrs. Caswell already seated at a table. There was also a young man, who appeared about the same age as Nellie, sitting with them.

"Mr. and Mrs. Caswell, allow me to introduce my traveling companion, Abigail," Nellie announced formally.

Mrs. Caswell nodded in acknowledgment toward Abigail. "May I present my nephew, Henry Caswell. He will accompany us to Liverpool." Mrs. Caswell seemed to say this disapprovingly. Henry looked down at his plate. Abigail and Nellie sensed that there must have been a dispute prior to their arrival.

"I am pleased to make your acquaintance, Mr. Caswell," Nellie said politely. Henry looked up at her. His dark eyes seemed tired and sad, but when he looked toward Nellie, she could see at once how handsome his features were. She was surprised that the Caswells could have had such an attractive relation, as they were not so much to look at themselves.

"And I am pleased to make yours," he answered in a deep voice.

The dinner was eaten with the usual pleasantries exchanged, but it was clear that Henry was not in the good graces of the Caswells. They acted as if they only tolerated his presence.

Nellie and Abigail returned to the hotel suite after dinner. "Well, that was odd," she commented. "I did not know the Caswells were bringing their nephew. What did you think of him?"

"He was quiet," Abigail replied.

"Yes, he was. Abigail, what do you think of the stable boy at Davenport House?" Nellie asked, abruptly changing the subject.

Abigail unknowingly held her breath and felt her face burning. "I think he is kind," she exhaled, thinking it was a safe enough answer. Abigail was aware that Nellie had fancied Ethan for years, but Abigail was beginning to fall in love with him, herself.

"Did you know that I once asked Father if I could marry him?" Nellie resumed with a giggle. "Father said no, of course. But I do believe that Ethan is terribly handsome. He will make a lady very fortunate one day."

"Indeed he will," Abigail agreed, hoping that it was the end of the questions about Ethan.

"Now tell me, what is happening between Mary and that Dr. Hamilton?" Nellie prodded.

Abigail hesitated. "I am sorry, but it is not my place to tell."

"Then she is in love with him," Nellie sighed as if Abigail had answered her question. "Do you think that Mary could be happy as a doctor's wife? I always thought that she would marry a gentleman. I do wish for Mary to be happy of course, but I will be disappointed when she is wed. It will mean that my friends will have no time to see me. That is what happens when girls get married, you know. They stop speaking to their friends who do not have husbands."

"I did not know," Abigail responded.

"It is true. But let us not worry about that now. Let us prepare to go to the theater. Our play will start soon and we have the best seats in the house! I am certain you will love *A Midsummer Night's Dream*!"

Abigail enjoyed the play immensely and both girls later retired to their suite at the hotel, only to fall asleep quickly and dream of the adventure yet to come.

The next morning, Pier 54 in New York was teeming with excited travelers. The Caswells left the hotel before Nellie and Abigail, so the girls hired their own carriage to take them through the chaotic traffic. When they came into view of the ship, Abigail appeared as if she might be about to cry. Nellie did all that she could to make Abigail feel comfortable about boarding the imposing vessel.

The third class passengers formed a noisy crowd of people of all ages. Some of the foreign ones appeared to be suffering from illness. Nellie wondered if they were being sent back to Europe after being deemed unfit to stay in America. She heard that it happened with many immigrants. "This way for the first-class passengers, Abigail," she said, gently taking her elbow and steering her toward the correct boarding area.

They had nearly reached the stairs to board the ship, when Abigail gasped suddenly. "Nellie! Ethan is here!" She pointed him out to Nellie.

Nellie looked over in surprise. It was true. There in the crowd, held back by the pier guards, stood the Davenport's stable boy. "What on earth is Ethan doing here?" Nellie wondered aloud, and stepped out of the way so the other passengers could move past her. "I will hold our place here. Go see what he wants, quickly." When Abigail was speaking with Ethan, Nellie looked on in bewilderment to see that Mary's friend Dr. Hamilton was with him.

When Abigail returned to report to Nellie, she looked frightened. "Is that Mary's Dr. Hamilton?" asked Nellie in surprise. "I cannot imagine what he can be doing here just now."

Abigail tried to speak with Nellie discreetly. "They have come to stop us. Dr. Hamilton said that our ship is a target for the War and we are putting our lives at risk by boarding it today."

"Oh, all of the rumors," Nellie said casually. "Dear Abigail, they would not continue with this voyage if it was unsafe. Look at all of these people. Do you think that they would board the ship if they believed those rumors? We needn't worry. The crew know what they are doing."

"I really think we should listen to them," Abigail persisted.

"Oh, I will go to talk to Dr. Hamilton myself. Hold our place in line so that we may board in a moment." Nellie went over to Dr. Hamilton and Ethan who stood a distance away to wait for them. "You two are scaring poor Abigail," she scolded. "Why have you come all this way today?"

Dr. Hamilton looked her in the face solemnly. "The German Embassy has warned Americans not to sail on this ship. Some suspect that there are weapons aboard being transported to Great Britain, which makes your ship a target. I beg of you not to go. Postpone your journey for another time when it is safe."

"I cannot postpone. It has all been arranged. I am afraid you have wasted your trip here. We will not be in

London very long," she assured him with a smile. "You will see us again in no time."

"Miss Whitmore," said Ethan anxiously. "Abigail will do whatever you say, even if it means putting her life at risk. If you will not listen to us, you must make it clear that it is her choice whether to go with you."

Nellie was touched by their concern, but she reasoned that the ship would not have boarded the passengers if what Dr. Hamilton and Ethan said was true. She returned to Abigail who stood waiting for her near the stairs. "I am going to board now, Abigail. You must decide whether to go with me or go back to Davenport House with the men. I know that the doctor is worried for us, but I think he is overly cautious. Still, you must do what your heart tells you and not worry whose feelings you may hurt," Nellie spoke compassionately. Abigail nodded. The girls got back in line and showed their documents to the crew. Ethan and Dr. Hamilton looked on in sorrow.

But when Abigail took the first step onto the stairs she cried out. "Wait! Nellie, I can't. I am sorry!"

Nellie tried to swallow her disappointment and responded kindly. "Do what you must, Dear. Do not worry about me." She kissed Abigail on the cheek and watched her leave the boarding area. Then Nellie felt a tear roll down her face as she took the remaining steps and realized that she would be taking the voyage alone.

Chapter 2

Lucy Whitmore wore a long black dress and long expression, exactly as she had the last three years since she became widowed. She was in the drawing room of her London home, sitting at a secretary desk and sealing an envelope. She tried to calmly hand the letter to her maid who was standing nearby. "Please post this immediately, Julia," Lucy ordered.

Julia glanced at the name on the letter and stared back at Lucy with wide eyes. "Are you certain, Madam?"

Lucy looked impatiently at Julia. "Come now, Julia. It has been three years. I should be able to invite whomever I please to my house. It is my niece's soiree, after all."

Julia nodded obediently and left the room with the letter. Lucy breathed a sigh of relief that she was alone in the room once more. She looked down at her hands that were still shaking from nerves. She even considered following Julia to retrieve the letter before it could be sent, but instead took several deep breaths, convincing herself to stay at her desk, as if nothing unusual had happened at all.

Captain Frederick Perry was absorbed in a book in his study when the letter arrived. "Post for you, Captain," announced his footman. Frederick grunted in response and the footman placed the letter on the desk as usual. After finishing the passage he was reading, Frederick glanced uninterested at the envelope on the desk. Then he did a double-take. The book that he held dropped loudly to the floor. He continued to stare at the letter with wide eyes and began to circle the desk only gazing at it, as if afraid to touch it. He finally reached for the letter and tore it open so quickly that it nearly ripped in two.

"Lucy," he sputtered in disbelief. He called for the footman to order the car and was soon on his way to St. John's Wood in London.

"Madam!" Julia cried in a whisper.

Lucy was still at the desk in her drawing room and startled from her daydream when Julia walked in. "What is it, Julia?"

"He is here!" the maid whispered frantically.

"Who?" Lucy asked bewildered.

"Captain Perry!"

Lucy's eyes grew wide and her mouth hung open. "Here is here? Now?"

Julia nodded. "He waits in the front hall."

Lucy felt her heart racing in her chest and she held onto the desk for support. "Tell him I'll be right down, Julia," she replied more confidently than she felt. She stood up and smoothed out her dress before walking carefully down the stairs to the hall. When Lucy saw the captain, she nearly stumbled, and was only grateful that her faltering knees were hidden by her dress. The man standing before her looked just as frazzled as she felt, yet he beamed a large smile.

"Lucy!" he greeted as she approached.

"Frederick! Um—I am terribly sorry, I meant to say—Captain Perry," Lucy corrected herself quickly. "I was not expecting to see you so soon."

Frederick laughed. "It has been twenty years. How can any time be too soon? When I saw that the letter was written in your hand, I came straight away. You surprised me, Lucy! An invitation from you after all these years!"

"Well yes—but—" she stammered. "The party is not for another week. It is for my niece."

"Then consider my visit today as my promise to attend," he said proudly. "I still cannot believe it."

Lucy turned her face away. She could not look into his eyes a minute longer. "Thank you, Captain Perry. I will confirm your attendance to the staff." From the corner of her vision she could see that he still stood there expectantly. Lucy wondered what he was waiting for. Part of her wished that he would leave already.

"Is that all?" Frederick asked. "Have you nothing more to say to me?"

Lucy looked up and met his gaze. "I only thought you might like to come to the party. My niece will be visiting from America."

Frederick nodded with a sigh. "I see. When does your niece arrive?"

"She arrives Thursday, on the ocean liner called Lusitania."

Frederick's expression changed quickly to concern. "The Lusitania!"

Lucy raised her eyebrows in surprise. "What is wrong?"

Frederick looked solemn. "It is too early to say."

Lucy lowered herself into the settee in the hall, worried over receiving such an answer from a knowledgeable sea captain. "I am suddenly panicked. I never thought it would be a problem. Her father sounded so confident over the telegram. Surely he would not have sent her—if he had thought—"

"I am sorry to have worried you," Frederick said gently, regretting that his answer had worried Lucy. "Surely your niece will arrive on Saturday, as expected. Thank you for the invitation to the party. I am certain it will be a grand affair."

Lucy nodded, but still looked frightened.

"I will leave now," Frederick said. "You must have much to do to prepare for your niece's arrival. Goodbye, Lucy." He let himself out the door while Lucy remained in the settee, staring with worry.

"Please, God, let her be alright," she whispered.

Nellie was shown to her suite aboard the ship. The room was small compared to what she was used to, but usual for a ship stateroom and adequate for the week. The room had a writing desk and chest of drawers. A bed made with luxurious linens was set against the wall with a picture window, while an identically made bed was positioned on the opposite side of the room. Nellie was sad to see the second bed, feeling Abigail's absence more deeply now. She tipped the steward and walked over to the window of her room to look out. She could see the pier and wondered if Abigail was still there to watch the ship set sail. The people on the ground looked small like ants while they weaved through the lines to board the ship.

Nellie removed her hat and lay on the bed next to the window. She could soon hear muffled shouts of "bon voyage" from other passengers on the decks below. Nellie did not feel like watching the ship pull away. After lying in bed, she became restless and decided to have a walk around the ship. She walked down the narrow hallway away from her room, and observed that a man was walking in her direction from the other end of the hallway. She recognized him at once as the Caswell's nephew, but wondered if he remembered her since he had looked at his plate for most of dinner. Just as they were about to cross paths, Henry nodded toward Nellie. "Miss Whitmore," he said in his deep voice.

"Mr. Caswell," Nellie returned the greeting. Henry looked down at the floor and appeared as though he would walk past her without saying another word. "Um—please—Mr. Caswell?" she said before he could walk away.

Henry stopped walking and met her gaze. "Yes?" he asked.

Nellie could feel herself blushing and realized that she had not planned what to say next. It was not often that she was speechless, but this was one of those moments. "How do you like the ship?" she finally asked.

"It will get us to where we are going," he answered.

"Do you know your way around?"

"I am just exploring for now. Most of the public rooms are on the boat deck."

"I was about to explore as well," Nellie remarked. They stood there awkwardly while Nellie hoped that he would say something. When he remained silent, Nellie asked, "Would you mind if I walked with you?"

"Does your friend wish to accompany us?" Henry asked, motioning for Nellie to walk beside him.

"Abigail will not be coming. She decided to return to Pennsylvania, so now I am traveling alone." Nellie walked carefully down the hallway with Henry. It was a funny feeling to walk in the moving ship. Every now and then she could feel herself leaning to one side or the other. Henry seemed polite enough, and Nellie did not feel speechless anymore. She gladly filled the silence with her chatter. "We were stopped at the pier by some friends of ours. They had come to warn us about boarding the ship, and Abigail went back with them. We are not really in danger, are we?"

Henry was quiet to the point that Nellie was not sure if he would answer her at all. "I suppose you mean on account of the War," he replied at last. "I hope we are not in danger. It would be irresponsible for the captain to set sail today, if that were the case."

"Why are your aunt and uncle upset with you? Have you done something terrible?" Nellie blurted.

Henry chuckled. "You Americans just say what you are thinking, don't you?"

"Not all Americans," Nellie giggled. "Sometimes I do not realize what I have said until after I have said it. Forgive me, Mr. Caswell. We can talk about the weather, if you'd prefer."

Henry laughed again. "I am sorry for my mood, which has been unusually dismal as of late. You may as well start calling me Henry. We will be on the same boat for the next six days after all."

"And you may call me Nellie. Oh, I am so glad to have made a friend already! I was worried that I would be bored the whole voyage." They soon entered the first class lounge. It was an expansive room with stained glass windows and high ceilings. Henry motioned for Nellie to sit across from him in front of the green marble fireplace. Nellie glanced around the lounge in delight. "I do love this room. They've done a perfect job on this ship. The last one I took to Britain was not so fancy."

"Is your family in Britain now?" asked Henry.

"My parents are sending me to my aunt who lives in London," she answered. "We live in Lancaster, but my father is mad that I have not married yet. He thinks I am too old to be unmarried, so he is hoping my aunt's matchmaking skills can be put to good use for me."

Henry smiled, but did not dare ask the question. "You cannot be so old," he said.

"I am twenty. My friend Mary is twenty-two and she has not married yet. Although I do believe she will soon, making me the old maid of my social circle."

Henry shook his head. "I don't know why you ladies worry about such things. Men do not care when they marry. I am twenty but I do not feel too old."

"It is because you are a man. You could be sixty and marry a girl of eighteen years. No one would think anything of it. But If I was sixty and wanted to marry a man of eighteen years, it would be nothing short of vulgar."

Henry stifled a laugh. "But you have a beauty about you that will still show through at sixty, surely."

Nellie giggled. "If I should live to be so old. I have not given much thought to marriage for myself. There was a time that I would tease Father that I wanted to marry a stable boy. You can imagine his reaction to that."

"Yes, I can," Henry replied. "I thought that all ladies were in a hurry to marry. It seems that some ladies think it is their only purpose in life."

Nellie paused thoughtfully. "Yes, I suppose some do. But they also talk about marrying for love, and I am not sure I believe in it. Do you think there is such a thing?"

Henry shrugged. "I only know that I do not like being sent here and there and told who my wife will be. The reason I was in America is because my parents arranged for me to marry a girl in New York. When I finally met her in person, I refused. So to answer your question, that is why my aunt and uncle are cross with me."

"Was the girl not to your liking?" Nellie asked curiously.

"On the contrary, she was beautiful and kind. It is why I refused her. She deserved better than me."

"You speak as if it would be punishment for the girl to marry you," Nellie said.

"It would be, in my circumstances. My father selected this girl because her family has a vast fortune—a fortune that my father wishes for our family to take control of. I did not think it right to marry a girl under such pretense. Do you think it is right?"

"I suppose not, but it is the way things are done," Nellie answered. "It has happened to me countless times—suitors coming to me for my family's money, I mean. I dismissed them all without a second thought. I would rather enjoy life than marry only for the sake of it."

Henry smiled. "I am glad to hear it."

Nellie turned her head to look around the room when their conversation reached a pause. Then she looked down at her dress and giggled. "I forgot that I would be wearing these old clothes until my traveling cases are delivered. They are not at all suitable for dinner."

"I'm certain they are fine," said Henry. "No one changes clothes on the first night of a voyage anyway. Or if you'd like, you could have dinner in your suite, like I plan to."

Nellie blinked in confusion. "How do you mean?"

Henry laughed. "Sorry, I meant to say that I will have dinner sent to my room. And you could request that your dinner is sent to your room."

"You won't dine with your aunt and uncle this evening?"

Henry shook his head. "You saw what last night's dinner was like. I intend to make myself scarce around them for the remainder of the voyage."

"You could explain to them why you refused the girl, as you explained to me."

"They would not be so understanding. You were able to refuse your suitors—but people in my family are never given the option. My aunt married my uncle being under the impression that he would be heir to our castle and title. My father was the oldest born, but he was expected to pass away before he lived to have children. That would have made my uncle the new heir. To my aunt's disappointment, Father is still alive today. And of course, I am his heir now. My aunt and uncle have more than one reason to dislike me, you see."

"How depressing it must be to marry on such terms, only to be disappointed in the end," Nellie pondered. "Wait, do you mean that you live in a castle?"

Henry sighed. "Indeed."

Nellie laughed. "A proper English castle? You must be nobility as well. Was I supposed to address you as Lord Henry?"

"Don't you dare. In fact, if you begin calling me Lord anything, I will stop speaking to you this moment," he teased with a twinkle in his eye.

"Very well," Nellie replied, her own green eyes shining. "Then you are a paradox. A lord who does not wish to be called a lord, who turns down a lovely rich lady because she is lovely and rich. What is it that you want in life, if not the grand life you have already?"

"No one has asked me before," Henry answered. "I want to be a doctor. I want to help people so that my life might mean something. I hope that I am remembered for more than an entry in Burke's Peerage."

"How wonderful! Have you studied medicine?"

He frowned. "Not officially. I have studied every text that I could get my hands on, but my father never allowed my admission into medical school. Did you know there are great advances in medicine from the East? Only, the methods are not new but centuries old. My father calls it sorcery, but I think there is something to it."

Nellie smiled. She did not know how to respond, but she enjoyed watching Henry tell of his ambitions.

"I am sorry, I have been speaking of myself for too long. You are a paradox as well, Nellie. You are a lady who does not care if she marries. I did not know such a thing existed. I suppose that you do not have a need to, since you are an American heiress."

Nellie forced a smile, but decided to change the subject. "Does your castle have a moat?" she asked abruptly.

"It does. I have considered renaming our home 'Mosquito Castle' because of it."

Nellie laughed again. She had thought Henry to be so serious when they first met. Now that they conversed in the lounge, Nellie realized that Henry was as funny as he was delightful for company. It began to get late, even though it felt as if they had only spoken for a few minutes.

"I should be going to dinner now," Nellie excused herself sheepishly. "It would be rude of me to not dine with my chaperons tonight. They did offer to see me safely to London, after all."

Henry smiled. "Of course. I enjoyed chatting with you this afternoon, Nellie. As you say, it is good to have a friend aboard."

"It is, and thank you. Goodbye, Henry."

Nellie later arrived at the first class dining room. The raised dome ceiling was painted in marvelous frescoes, and both levels of the dining room exuded neoclassical luxury. Nellie and the Caswells were seated in the upper level with a balcony view into the lower level.

"Why has Abigail not come to dinner?" inquired Mrs. Caswell.

"Oh—I am afraid that she did not board the ship with me this morning. Abigail decided to return to her home in Pennsylvania."

"How ungrateful of her. Isn't she here as your companion? I hope you did not pay her allowance in advance," commented Mrs. Caswell.

"I do not think she was being ungrateful. She became frightened over rumors of the War and turned back at the last minute," Nellie explained.

"I see. I am sorry for you then, Nellie. You must have been bored out of your mind waiting for dinner with us tonight. We met a family today with a girl your age who is also from Lancaster. Do you know a Priscilla Campbell?"

Nellie's eyes lit up. "Why, yes I do! I had no idea that Priscilla would be on this voyage. You have made my day!"

Mrs. Caswell smiled. "Then you will have a friend aboard after all. Priscilla appears to be a lovely girl who can keep you proper company. She said she will spend most of the voyage in the reading room."

"Yes, she does love her books," Nellie responded. "I will look for her first thing tomorrow."

CHAPTER 3

The next morning, a steward brought the traveling cases to Nellie's room. After he unpacked Nellie's case, the steward was about to unpack Abigail's case which he also brought with him. "That won't be necessary," Nellie said quickly, trying to hide her sadness. "Just put that one under the bed for now." The steward obeyed and left the room. Nellie was grateful to have her choice of clothes again. She got dressed and went to the reading room after breakfast. She immediately recognized her friend who was sitting near a window. "Priscilla!" Nellie whispered excitedly.

Priscilla looked up from the book she was reading. "Nellie?" she responded in surprise.

"Oh, I am so glad you are here! My chaperons told me that they met your family yesterday," Nellie replied.

Priscilla still appeared to be in shock that Nellie was there, but managed to speak. "Yes, I am going to stay with my cousins in Brighton for the rest of the year."

"But how have you been?" asked Nellie as she sat down beside her. "I have not seen you in ages."

Priscilla looked down at the floor. "I have been well," she answered slowly.

"What is the matter? You do not look like yourself."

"You think I look different?" Priscilla asked suddenly.

"I mean you do not seem happy to see me," Nellie admitted. "Is everything alright?"

"I am happy to see you, Nellie. I'm afraid that I am not feeling well today. It must be the motion of the ship."

"I am sick from the motion sometimes too, but so far this has been a smooth sailing. I am sorry you are not feeling well."

Priscilla forced a smile. "Did you come in here just to find me?"

"Of course I did. I hoped that we could keep each other company this week."

"I would like that," Priscilla replied. She closed her book and joined Nellie to explore the other decks of the ship. They enjoyed looking through the glass wall of the lift going up and down to the different floors. Priscilla did not seem to be having much fun and excused herself to retire to her room. Nellie was left alone once more, walking through the narrow hallways until finally settling into a sofa in the lounge. She sat near the green fireplace as she had the day before, in the hopes that Henry might find her and they could have another conversation. All through the day, Nellie expected see him, but it seemed as though she was only seeing the same twenty passengers over and over. Nellie had dinner with her chaperons that night, disappointed that she did not see Henry or Priscilla again. She hoped that she would see them both the next day.

On the third day of the voyage, Nellie found Priscilla in the reading room again. Priscilla appeared to be getting up as if to leave. "Oh, good afternoon, Nellie," she said. Even though her greeting was polite, Priscilla seemed distressed.

"Dear Priscilla, are you feeling ill again? Here, come with me to my suite. You can lie down on the bed. My room is so much closer than yours is down all those stairs."

Priscilla nodded and they both went to Nellie's room where Priscilla immediately lay upon the bed. "Your room is lovely. Thank you for bringing me here. I was worried that I might faint."

"Perhaps we should ask the ship doctor to see you," Nellie suggested. "I am worried for you. The sea swells will be worst than this in the coming days."

Priscilla began to cry. "It is not the sea that is making me feel this way."

Nellie carefully sat on the bed beside her friend. "Please don't cry. Tell me what is wrong. Clearly you are upset about something. Can I help?"

"There is no help for what is happening to me," Priscilla said through her tears. "Mother and Father will hardly speak to me. My sisters despise me. I only want to be home in Lancaster, but I have to be on this voyage instead."

"But why is your family being awful to you? You could never deserve such treatment."

"I'm afraid that I deserve it, and more. I am now disgraced. I planned to run away with Edward, you see—and I would have if my parents did not stop me."

"Edward?" Nellie asked, trying to think of who Priscilla could mean. Then she asked, "Edward Vanderbilt?"

"No—Edward Brown," Priscilla replied mournfully. "Our butler."

Nellie's mouth hung open. "My word, Priscilla—the family butler! Your father must have raked him over the coals!"

"He did, and I have not seen Edward since. I miss him so terribly," Priscilla sobbed.

"You must care for him very much," Nellie sympathized, putting her arm around her friend.

"But Nellie, it is a hundred times worse than what I have just told you," she cried.

"How can it be worse?"

"I am pregnant."

Nellie felt her arm fall to her side. She tried to not appear as shocked as she felt. "How did this happen?" she whispered with wide eyes.

"We were planning to marry before anything happened, but—I cannot explain it. When you love someone, it causes you to do the most drastic things you never thought possible. Edward does not know about the baby, and now he never will." Priscilla sighed as if her confession had lifted a weight from her shoulders. "Nellie, tell me the truth…do you hate me now?"

"I am surprised. But I could not hate you over such a thing," Nellie assured her.

"You won't tell anyone, will you?"

"I won't say a word. But—should you be traveling in your condition?"

"It is because of my condition that I am traveling. I am expected to stay in Brighton for my time of confinement, then return to Lancaster after the baby is born. As if nothing had ever happened."

Nelly's eyes grew wider. "Without the baby?"

Priscilla nodded. "I can never recover from this. I've nearly thrown myself over the side because of my misery. I must see Edward again, or I will die."

Nellie thought quietly for a while, not knowing what to say to help her friend's sorrow. "If there is anything I can do…" Nellie trailed off, seeing that Priscilla appeared ready to fall asleep.

"Please, continue to be my friend," she whispered. "I need a friend desperately now."

"Of course," Nellie answered. "I will receive you at my aunt's house in London as often as I am able. She is having a party for me, you know. You must come. I will add your name to the guest list as soon as I arrive at the house."

"It sounds lovely," Priscilla replied sleepily.

"Why don't you rest now. I will bring you some water." Nellie stood up to pour her friend a glass, but before she could return with the water, Priscilla had already fallen sleep.

Nellie quietly slipped out of the room and headed again to the first class lounge. She scanned the room near the green fireplace, but saw no sign of Henry. Disappointed, she returned to her suite where Priscilla was just beginning to wake.

"Oh dear, did I fall asleep?" she asked when Nellie walked in.

Nellie giggled. "You must have been very tired. It is time to change for dinner now. Would you like to dine with my chaperons and me tonight?"

Priscilla sighed. "I wish I could, but my parents expect me to dine with them. I appreciate the invitation. Thank you for being a friend, Nellie."

"Of course. I hope to see you again tomorrow. Perhaps we can meet at the veranda cafe at noon? If you are not feeling too tired."

"It is a wonderful plan. I will be there." Priscilla left the room and Nellie began to change for dinner. She wore white evening gloves with her green floor-length gown.

When she arrived at the Caswell's usual dining table, she felt her heart flutter suddenly in her chest. Mr. and Mrs. Caswell were not there. But Henry was.

"Good evening," he greeted Nellie as he stood up to pull her chair out for her. Then he laughed. "I forget these chairs are bolted to the floor. It is not going anywhere."

Nellie giggled as she lowered herself into her seat. "I am surprised to see you here. Have you resolved things with your aunt and uncle?"

Henry shook his head. "Not at all. But I was worried that I might never see you unless I came to dinner. I thought that we might cross paths today in the ship, but you must have spent the day in your room."

Nellie's mouth hung open indignantly. "I thought it was you who hid in your room all day! I did not see you once, and I have roamed about the ship throughout the afternoon."

Henry chuckled. "Impossible. I even waited by the green fireplace in case you came back."

"You didn't! I waited there for you myself!" Both Nellie and Henry were laughing now, not entirely sure if the other was teasing or being truthful.

"I thought you must have found another friend to keep you company," Henry said.

"As a matter of fact, I have discovered that a friend of mine from America is on this voyage. I did spend the afternoon with her today and we will meet again tomorrow."

"I am glad for you," Henry was saying, just as Mr. and Mrs. Caswell arrived at the table.

"Please forgive our tardiness. There was a mix-up with our luggage and we have not had our cases until now—"

Mrs. Caswell stopped when she noticed Henry. "Oh. Good evening, Henry."

"Good evening, Aunt," Henry replied, rising from his seat. He smiled wryly at Nellie before turning to Mrs. Caswell. "Here, let me get the chair for you." Nellie stifled a giggle.

"That won't be necessary," Mrs. Caswell scowled, maintaining her distance from Henry. Mr. Caswell was silent as usual as he took his seat. The only time he spoke was when the waiter came by with the menu. Nellie made sure to fill any awkward silence with the story of how she and Priscilla had been exploring the ship. The others did not speak much during the meal, and Mr. and Mrs. Caswell left right after dinner to retire to bed. Nellie and Henry remained at the table for another cup of tea.

"You were brave to attend this dinner," teased Nellie.

"It was worth it," Henry shrugged.

Nellie blushed. "I am glad you came tonight. Do you think you will dine with us again tomorrow?"

Henry cringed. "If I cannot find you elsewhere, I just might have to. It is the only way I can have a decent conversation on this ship."

"I am flattered," Nellie laughed. "I can meet you before dinner tomorrow, if you'd like. Then your aunt will not be scowling at you the whole time you are trying to eat."

"I would like that," said Henry. "By the green fireplace?"

"Yes, by the green fireplace."

"I will be there. Good night, Nellie."

"Good night, Henry."

Chapter 4

Nellie met Priscilla at the veranda cafe. The sea was becoming choppier and causing the ship to rock more than it had since leaving New York. "I don't know how much more of this I can take!" cried Priscilla, gripping the edges of the table.

"It does seem to be worse today," Nellie remarked. Many of the passengers had expressed worry about how much the ship was rocking, but the captain assured them that it was normal for the north Atlantic. Nellie observed that there were not many people on the deck. It was then that she saw a little girl who appeared about three years old, but looked quite out of place near the cafe. "Look over there, Priscilla. Do you think she is lost?" Nellie pointed to the little girl.

"She is certainly not a first class passenger," Priscilla replied, noticing the ragged state of the girl's clothing.

Nellie looked around to see if the child's parents might be watching from afar, but there was no one around just then. "We should find a steward so she can be returned to her family. I worry for her being up here alone while the boat is rocking so badly."

Priscilla agreed and went with Nellie to approach the girl. "Where is your mother, Dear?"

"Downstairs," the girl answered.

"We are going to return you to your family now. Alright?" Nellie smiled. The child nodded and Nellie took her hand, guiding her toward the stairs that joined the decks of the ship. "If we find a steward, he will know where to take her." But they did not find anyone who could help as they descended the grand staircase. "Perhaps we should take her directly to the third class rooms."

"By ourselves?" questioned Priscilla.

"Have you seen anyone who could help? We cannot leave her wandering by herself," Nellie reasoned. They left the comforts of the first class section to find the common room in the forward end of the ship. A large open room with long tables and bar stools appeared to be where the third class passengers congregated. When Nellie and Priscilla walked in, the passengers stopped what they were doing and stared at them. Nellie was just about to announce what they were doing there when a teenage girl stepped out from the crowd.

"Charlotte is found!" she exclaimed. "The ladies brung her, just as the old woman predicted!" Some in the crowd began to clap and cheer as the girl approached to take the child's hand. "Thank you, Ma'am. She's my sister."

"Oh, I am glad we have found you! We discovered her wandering the boat deck and wanted to be sure she was with her family," Nellie explained. Priscilla stood there awkwardly. This common room was loud and plain, a stark contrast to the quiet lounges upstairs.

"When we couldn't find Charlotte, our mum asked the Gypsy woman where she could be. The woman predicted that two ladies from first class would bring her back," the girl told Nellie.

Nellie's eyebrows were raised in surprise. "How could she possibly know such a thing?"

"She tells fortunes for a tuppence. Come, I'll take you to her," the girl replied happily. Nellie smiled at Priscilla and began to follow the girl.

"Nellie, a fortune teller! We must leave immediately!" Priscilla whispered frantically, yet continued to follow Nellie through the room.

"I've never had my fortune told before, have you?" Nellie asked. "Perhaps she can tell about your dear Edward."

"But Nellie, it is sinful! I am in enough trouble as it is!" Priscilla argued. "We must return upstairs, away from these people."

"I cannot be so very sinful, if she was right about the lost child. I wish for her to tell my fortune. You may go back upstairs, if you wish," Nellie decided.

Priscilla looked around her in dismay. She did not want to walk through all those people alone. "I will stay with you, but please hurry."

They were led to an elderly woman seated in the corner of the room. A man stood next to her. The teenage girl turned to the man and said, "Look, Charlotte was found, just as your mother said."

The man smiled. "Very good," he said in a thick accent.

The girl gestured toward Nellie and Priscilla. "These ladies want to hear their fortunes."

The man turned to speak to his mother before nodding to Nellie and Priscilla. "My mother does not speak English. I will translate. She needs your hand."

Nellie took two silver coins from her purse and gave

them to the woman, who then handed the coins to her son. She took Nellie's hand and closed her eyes. A small crowd gathered around the girls to watch. When the old woman spoke, her son translated. "She sees a handsome man." Laughs and whispers went through the crowd while Nellie giggled to herself and gave Priscilla a look.

The old woman spoke again and everyone looked eagerly toward the son to hear his translation. "She sees a castle with water all around." The others in the crowd began laughing and whispering again, but Nellie turned serious and suddenly felt her heart pounding.

"What else does she see?" she asked anxiously. But the Gypsy woman released Nellie's hand.

"She sees no more," the man explained.

"But I must hear more," Nellie said, bringing out her coin purse again.

The man shook his head. "I'm sorry, Miss. It's all my mother has for you."

Nellie was disappointed and turned to Priscilla. "I'm sorry. We can go back now."

Priscilla hesitated. "Perhaps I will have my fortune told after all," she said nervously. Nellie was happy to hear this and watched as the old woman took her friend's hand. But the woman shrieked and dropped Priscilla's hand immediately. She spoke to her son aggressively, then rose from her seat and walked away. The man called after her, but his mother refused to listen. The crowd was murmuring again.

"I'm sorry, Miss," the man said, looking helplessly at Priscilla. "My mother said she will not give anymore fortunes today. Here is your coin back."

"You may keep it, but what did she say before she left? Why did she let go of my hand?" Priscilla questioned.

The man looked pained as he answered her question. "My mother said, 'ice cold'."

"What does that mean?" begged Priscilla, her eyes growing wide with fear.

"I don't know, Miss. I'm sorry."

Nellie could suddenly feel the boat strongly rocking under her feet again. "Let us go back upstairs," she urged Priscilla. They went back to Priscilla's room and sat upon the beds.

"What did she mean when she said ice cold?" asked Priscilla.

Nellie cringed. "I'm afraid it was wrong of me to insist that we have our fortunes told. I did not realize it would be so upsetting. Forgive me, please," Nellie apologized.

"Do you think there is anything to it?"

"I don't know what to think. Perhaps she was tired and did not wish to continue. Please do not worry about what the Gypsy woman said, or I will feel dreadful for having persuaded you."

Priscilla sighed heavily. "I am so tired. I think I should try to sleep before dinner."

Nellie managed a smile. "I will leave so you can rest. Would you like me to bring you anything?"

"No, I am alright," replied Priscilla. Her eyes were closed and it looked as if she was already drifting off to sleep.

Nellie walked out of the room and quietly closed the door behind her. She then remembered that she told Henry she would meet him before dinner. She walked to the lounge and saw him sitting near the fireplace, watching the flames. He rose from his seat and smiled. "Nellie, good afternoon."

"Good afternoon," she greeted quietly.

"What is it? You look as if you've seen a ghost," remarked Henry.

"Something peculiar happened today. My friend and I had our fortunes told by a woman from Rumania. She scared Priscilla by what she said," Nellie explained.

"What did the woman say to her?" he questioned.

"She hardly said anything at all, only enough to scare Priscilla. Now I feel terrible, because I persuaded her to hear the old woman."

"I am sure there is nothing to worry about. The woman likely only wanted more money to give a better fortune," suggested Henry.

"It is what I thought too, but she would not take more money from us. In fact, her son tried to return the coin."

Henry appeared thoughtful for a moment. "What fortune did the woman give to you?"

Nellie was startled by his question and not sure if she wanted to answer. "Oh—" she sputtered. "It was—nothing important."

"How did you even find this woman? You have me curious now," said Henry.

Nellie sighed. "She was in the common room. In third class."

Henry smiled in amusement. "What on earth were you doing in third class?"

"Oh," smiled Nellie. "A little girl from there had wandered up to the boat deck and we returned her to her family. That was how we learned of the fortune teller. Apparently, she foretold that two ladies from first class would return the girl. And that is what happened. So you must see why

Priscilla would be concerned over what this woman had to say."

The ship rocked hard to one side just then, causing Nellie to fall forward from her seat. Henry caught her before she hit the ground. "Are you alright? The swells are getting rather high," he said.

"I am beginning to feel sick. I think I should return to my room," Nellie answered. She tried to steady herself on the rocking ship.

"Please, let me walk you there," insisted Henry. They walked through the hallways quickly because neither of them knew how sick Nellie was about to be. The ship jerked to one side again, sending both of them into the wall.

"This is terrible!" cried Nellie. Tears were beginning to form in her eyes as her stomach turned this way and that.

"Try to breathe in through your nose, then exhale through your mouth," Henry suggested.

Nellie tried to do as he said, but it did not ease the feeling in her stomach. They finally made it to the door of her suite and Nellie leaned her back against the door, closing her eyes and taking deep breaths before trying to go in, wishing the boat would stay still long enough for her to do so.

Henry stood across from her. "I would like to try something that I learned in a book, if you will permit me."

"What is it?" Nellie asked wearily, opening her eyes.

"If I may take your hand for a moment, there are locations to press on that may ease your symptoms."

"Alright," Nellie agreed, holding out her hand.

Henry carefully took her hand in his and Nellie felt a surge of electricity course through her arm, sending her heart racing in her chest. "Oh, I feel something happening!" she exclaimed, momentarily forgetting her sickness.

Henry laughed and said quietly, "Nellie, I haven't done anything yet."

"Oh," she replied, swallowing her embarrassment.

"You just press here on top of the wrist," he said while showing her. "And up here on the other side. Hold for a few seconds. Then release." He looked in her eyes. "Do you feel any different?"

"I am not certain," Nellie replied. "What should I be feeling?"

Henry chuckled. "I am not certain either. The sea does not make me ill, so I have wanted to observe this technique on someone else to see if there is any truth to it. I suppose we won't know just yet."

Nellie turned around and opened her door. "Thank you for trying, anyway. I think I will go lie down for a while. I will have dinner sent to my room tonight."

"I hope to see you again tomorrow," Henry told her.

"I hope so too," she said, smiling at him once more before she closed the door.

Lucy Whitmore was seated at the breakfast table in her London home when her maid brought a letter on a silver tray. "Post for you, Madam," stated Julia.

Lucy read the letter with interest. "It is a reply from the Duke of Staffordshire," she smiled. "His Grace will attend the soiree. I am delighted to receive this news, for he appeared quite taken with my niece when he last saw her. Thank goodness he is still a bachelor. Nellie could be a duchess."

"Her parents are sure to be pleased, Madam," replied Julia.

Lucy sighed. "I do hope this party is a success. Nellie was so very stubborn about marriage when she was here before. It was almost as if she did not wish to marry. Can you imagine?"

"I cannot imagine," replied Julia.

"Is everything ready for her arrival?"

"I prepared Miss Nellie's room just this morning, Madam."

"And a room for her companion?"

"It is prepared as well," answered Julia.

"Marvelous," said Lucy. "They will take the train from Liverpool with the Caswells tomorrow and I intend to meet with them at the station. We will not plan anything for the next few days while Nellie settles in. I have not crossed the sea myself, but I have heard that it can be very tiring."

"As you wish, Madam," answered Julia.

Nellie did not want to leave her bed that morning. The ship rocked hard, rising sharply with the swells and crashing back down again. Nellie managed to stand up long enough to look out of the picture window. She was alarmed when she saw the height of the crests, and immediately lay back down. The motion of the ship was only tolerable if Nellie was still on her back. She worried for how Priscilla must be feeling. Nellie also wished that she could see Henry again, but she did not know how to walk around the ship without becoming ill. She requested again that dinner be sent to her room and remained there for the day. When there was a knock at the door of her suite that evening, Nellie thought that it was a steward with her dinner tray.

"Henry!" Nellie greeted in surprise. "Good evening."

"Good evening," he replied, but a look of concern was evident in his face. "Are you well?"

"Not at all," Nellie answered. "I don't think I can leave

my room while the waves are this high. Thank goodness that today is our last day at sea!"

"That is what I have come to tell you, Nellie. The captain has announced that we will not arrive in Liverpool tomorrow, but instead be delayed for another day."

"Is it because of this terrible weather?" asked Nellie.

"He did not explain. Some think that the reason for the delay is because the captain is avoiding u-boats in the area."

"Oh, I see. I wonder if we should be worried," said Nellie.

Henry smiled. "We are not the first voyage to be delayed for a day. It will be fine, surely."

"I hope the news reaches my Aunt Lucy in time, or she will wonder why I am not at the train station tomorrow. She does worry often."

"Do you get along with your aunt better than I get along with mine?" asked Henry.

"Oh, indeed. Aunt Lucy is marvelous. But she is lonely, for she never had children of her own and is now a widow. She is always glad when I come to visit her."

"I am happy that your aunt is amiable. As you can imagine, I will not have such a warm welcome when I return home. In fact, I was grateful when I heard that this voyage would be delayed for another day. The captain could delay it a week, and that would be agreeable to me."

Nellie laughed. "But it would not be agreeable to the rest of the passengers."

Henry laughed too. "No, I expect it wouldn't be." Henry looked into the hallway just then and observed a steward heading toward Nellie's room with a wheeled cart. "Ah, I do believe your dinner is here. I will leave now."

"Thank you for telling me of the Captain's announcement," Nellie told him as he turned to leave.

"Of course. Enjoy the rest of your evening, Nellie." Henry went down the hallway and realized that he did not know where to go next. The lounge was mostly empty because passengers had either gone to dinner or stayed in their rooms. Henry sat down near the green fireplace. He was suddenly aware of how alone it felt to be there without his new friend. He watched the flames and let his thoughts wander. He thought about how strangely Nellie had reacted when he asked what the fortune teller told her. She had seemed to be open to him about everything until then, and Henry wondered what it was it was that she did not want him to hear.

Henry pondered this by the fire and soon rose from his seat. He left the lounge and descended the staircase to the lower floors. He was soon walking into the expansive common room in the third class section of the ship, receiving odd stares from the passengers there. One man approached him and questioned him gruffly. "You lost?"

Henry laughed. "I heard there was a fortune teller aboard and I wish to hear mine told."

The man looked Henry up and down. "That's usually for the womenfolk."

"Could you be so good as to point me in the right direction?" asked Henry.

The man shrugged. "Suit yourself. In that corner in the back," he said with a jerk of his head.

Henry thanked the man and headed toward the back corner. The crowd dispersed to make a path, watching Henry curiously as he approached the Gypsy woman.

"Might I have my fortune told?" he asked kindly.

The woman's son who stood beside her spoke up. "I'm sorry, Sir. My mother speaks no English."

"Can she see the future?" asked Henry.

The man nodded. "But she refuses to tell more fortunes until we arrive on land."

Henry looked skeptically at the woman's son. He was aware that fortune tellers might put on an act to obtain more payment from their customers. Henry retrieved ten silver coins from his pocket and held out his hand. "Would this be enough for one fortune?"

The man's eyes were wide as he stared at the coins. He then began speaking intensely to his mother in Rumanian. They appeared to be arguing about whether to take the money. Henry was beginning to believe that the woman truly did not wish to speak to him.

Finally the man spoke to Henry. "I have persuaded her to tell your fortune. Give her your hand and I will translate her words."

The woman seemed reluctant but took Henry's hand when he held it out to her. She then closed her eyes and a hush fell over the crowd that stood behind Henry. The woman was quiet for so long that Henry began to lose faith that she would say anything at all. Just as he was about to pull his hand away, the woman suddenly grabbed his forearm and held on tightly. Her eyelids fluttered open and when they did, the woman's milky gray eyes were staring straight into Henry's. He felt chills run over his body and the hair on the back of his neck stood on end. His heart raced in his chest as the woman tightened her grip on his arm. She continued to look fixedly into Henry's frightened eyes, and when her lips parted, the words were spoken in perfect English: "Save me, Doctor!"

CHAPTER 5

The next day, a murmur of disappointment was heard among the passengers of the Lusitania. Once again, the captain assured everyone that the delay was nothing to be worried about, and that the ship was only taking precautions. One consolation was that the sea had calmed that day and was no longer tossing the ship about as it had the previous days. At the veranda cafe, Nellie met up with Priscilla, who was feeling better that afternoon.

"I am glad that we may at least be together another day," Nellie stated to her friend.

"You are kind to me, Nellie. I was dreading this voyage with all of my heart, but your being here has made all the difference."

Nellie smiled. They had not spoken another word about the Gypsy woman and intentionally kept their conversations light. "Priscilla, tell me…do you know of a Henry Caswell?"

Priscilla sat thoughtfully for a moment. "I know of a Lord Henry Caswell, if you mean the son of the Marquess. I believe the family lives in Surrey in an ages old castle. Although I have heard that it is in dire need of modernization. There are rumors that it does not even have electric lights installed. Can you imagine? In 1915! And they, the most prominent family in the area. I have also heard it said that the family has lived a grander life than they can afford."

"How curious," Nellie replied. "I wonder if it is true. Have you met Henry before?"

Priscilla raised her eyebrow at Nellie. " 'Henry'?" she laughed. "You must be acquainted with him far better than I."

Nellie blushed. "I met him in New York before we boarded the ship. His aunt and uncle are my chaperons."

"Is he a passenger, then?" asked Priscilla. Nellie nodded in response. "So that is why you disappear so often. I have only met him the one time, but I could not forget such a handsome face."

"He is clever as much as he is handsome. We have exchanged some wonderful conversations," Nellie explained.

"I believe this is the first time I have seen you smitten," giggled Priscilla. "But Nellie, I don't think there will be any money left by the time he inherits. Has he expressed his intentions toward you?"

"He has not. I suppose I am getting ahead of myself by even mentioning him," Nellie admitted.

"If you married him, you would be a Countess, at least," Priscilla continued. "Your family's money would make up for any shortage on the Caswell's part."

Nellie cringed. "That may be a problem. You see, my mother is expecting a child, which means that my inheritance will be divided. And if the baby is a boy, my father has said that I will have nothing. It is why I am going to

London. My aunt is expected to find an advantageous marriage for me."

"I am sorry, Nellie. I had no idea. I hope that whoever your aunt chooses will meet with your approval."

Nellie looked up at her seriously. "What were your thinking when you decided to leave with your butler? Surely your father would have disinherited you for it. What were your plans for a living?"

Priscilla gave a slight shrug of her shoulders. "Edward has a farmhouse near Harrisburg. His family resides there now, and I thought that we could move in until other arrangements could be made."

"You? In a farmhouse?" Nellie laughed incredulously. "I can hardly believe my ears. You must love him very much."

"Of course I do, Nellie."

"What does it feel like to be in love?"

"When I was home with Edward, our love was a more wonderful feeling than I ever dreamed possible. But now it has turned into the most sorrowful pain. I feel as if a part of me is missing, and I feel the ache in my heart and my stomach each day that we cannot be together." Tears had formed in Priscilla's eyes and began to stream down her soft cheeks. "I do not know what to do now that I will be on the other side of the world, and forced to give up our child. Is there any escape from this misery that my parents have forced upon me?"

"I don't know," Nellie answered helplessly. "If there is anything I may do to help…"

"I know you will, Nellie," Priscilla replied. But she quietly wondered how anyone could help her at all.

After Priscilla retired to her room, Nellie hoped to see Henry around the boat deck. It was nearing time for dinner and Nellie could not find him in the lounge or other rooms. She returned to her stateroom and carefully packed her traveling cases. The passengers were instructed to have their luggage placed outside their staterooms before dinner on the last night. Nellie carefully chose the clothes she would wear and left for the dining room. She was pleased to see Henry sitting there, although something about him seemed different tonight. Mr. and Mrs. Caswell were also seated.

"Thank you for seeing me safely to London," Nellie thanked them politely.

"It has been our pleasure, Nellie," replied Mrs. Caswell for the both of them. "I am sorry there has not been more to do here, and that the weather was so terrible those days. We cannot wait to be back in Exeter."

"Exeter?" Nellie asked quizzically.

"Yes, Mr. Caswell and I reside in Exeter. Be sure to meet with us during debarkation tomorrow so we may arrive at the Liverpool train station together," Mrs. Caswell instructed.

Nellie looked at Henry. He appeared serious and anxious, much like he did the night they first met. "Will you be taking the train with us?" she asked him.

Henry opened his mouth to answer, but his aunt spoke before he could. "Henry will travel separately to his home in Surrey. This dinner is the last time we expect to see him."

Henry was looking directly into Nellie's eyes in a way that made her heart race. He looked like he wanted to say something, but remained silent. Nellie wanted to say something too, but all she could do was look back into his eyes. Mrs. Caswell looked them over curiously, sensing the tension that was present at the table. To everyone's surprise, Mr. Caswell spoke up. "Please give my sincerest regards to your father, Henry. It has been ages since I saw him last, but I intend to make a visit to the castle soon after we arrive in Exeter. It has been too long since your father and I were fishing on the estate."

Mrs. Caswell cast a glare at her husband after his remark, but he appeared unaffected. Henry seemed to perk up at his uncle's statement. "Thank you, Uncle. My father will be glad to hear it. We look forward to your visit."

"My aunt is arranging a party for me next week," Nellie said. "I hope I may send invitations to all of you."

"Of course we will attend," Mrs. Caswell replied, suddenly turning cheerful. "And if I know your Aunt Lucinda, I suspect that she has already arranged the perfect match for you."

Nellie giggled. "Yes, that does sound like Aunt Lucy." She then looked at Henry who was still staring at her intently. He forced a smile before looking down at his plate.

"I'm afraid I did not pack my things before dinner as I should have," Henry said abruptly. "Please, excuse me. I wish you all safe travels. Goodbye, Uncle. Goodbye, Nellie. It was a pleasure to meet you."

"Goodbye," Nellie responded slowly, disappointed that Henry was leaving so soon. She hoped that they might speak at the dinner table after Mr. and Mrs. Caswell had retired to bed. The Caswells left soon after Henry, and Nellie returned to her room, settling in for her last night aboard the ship.

Excitement was felt in the air the following day. The passengers were eager to set their feet on dry land again, and many looked forward to the loved ones they would soon be untied with. Nellie was glad to be able to meet with Priscilla for an early lunch in the Palm Lounge. Priscilla became so tired afterward that she returned to her room. Nellie scanned the first class rooms, looking for Henry again. It was soon announced by the captain that the coast of Ireland was visible from the port side. The passengers raced to the decks in anticipation, hungry for the sight of land after the week at sea. Nellie rushed to Priscilla's room to tell her the news. Priscilla was already lying in bed.

"The fog has cleared and we can see Ireland from the ship now. Come with me to see it," Nellie coaxed.

Priscilla sighed sleepily. "I am so very tired, Nellie. You go on without me."

"Are you certain?" she asked.

"I don't think I can keep my eyes open for another second…" Priscilla drifted off and was soon sleeping peacefully.

Nellie smiled at her friend and kissed her forehead. "Have a good rest, Dear Priscilla." Nellie slipped out of the room and went up to the deck to see the coast. She removed her hat and allowed the fresh sea air to breeze through her hair.

A woman stood there on the deck, holding her crying baby. "Look, we are almost home, Darling," she was cooing to the infant. The baby continued to cry while his mother bounced him gently on her hip. Nellie could not help but smile.

"I can take him for a moment, if you wish," she said to the woman.

The woman breathed in relief. "Thank you. My arms are very tired. He has gotten so big!"

Nellie giggled in delight when the woman handed the baby into her arms. "What a handsome lad he is already," she remarked. The baby stopped crying and looked curiously at Nellie as she bounced him lightly and walked along the deck. Then Nellie heard a familiar deep voice behind her.

"I see you have made a new friend."

Nellie turned around to see Henry. "Good afternoon!" she greeted cheerfully. "I was not sure that I would see you again."

"Thank goodness that was not the case," replied Henry with a twinkle in his eye.

The baby's mother soon stepped in and thanked Nellie for calming him down. She then took her baby and walked down the deck, admiring the view of the coast. Nellie sighed as she watched the woman walk away. "The little one was such a dear," Nellie remarked. "I would have held him for longer if his mother had let me."

"Indeed, he seemed a bundle of joy," Henry replied.

Nellie removed a paper from the pocket of her dress and gave it to Henry. "I have written my aunt's address and the time of the party next week. You will come, won't you? I was not sure you would receive a proper invitation in time."

Henry put the paper away in his jacket pocket but seemed to hesitate. Then he said, "If you wish me to attend, then of course I will come."

Nellie beamed. "I would like to hug you right now, but my mother made me promise not to make a spectacle of myself. She told me that the English do not appreciate embracing as Americans do."

Henry laughed. "I suppose it is not generally done, but there are exceptions to every rule."

Nellie smiled and stepped closer to him. She could feel her heart racing, looking into his eyes that were smiling back at her. Suddenly, the ship was thrust violently to the starboard side, casting Nellie, Henry, and the other passengers against the large glass windows of the ship.

"What was that!" cried Nellie. People all around were panicking, trying to understand what had happened. It was worse than the ship had ever rocked in the past days, but the sea appeared calm. Something was wrong. Soon they began to hear the words "u-boat" and "torpedo" and watched as the lifeboats began to be deployed. There was confusion as the passengers boarded the lifeboats despite the captain's assurance that the ship would be fine. Henry did not seem so sure.

"Nellie, I think we should get into a lifeboat," he said solemnly.

"But I cannot swim!" she cried back.

"I will find lifebelts for us. Wait here for me!" Henry rushed into the ship's doors and quickly returned with lifebelts. They slipped them on and stood behind the other passengers on their way into one of the lifeboats. An explosion was heard just then which shook the ship hard and caused people to scream. Some shouted that it was another torpedo. Henry and Nellie were now in the lifeboat, holding on tightly as it was lowered into the water. They watched in horror as other lifeboats around them flipped or fell into the sea as they were being lowered. The shrieks of those still running on the decks, searching for a lifeboat to board were heard loud in clear in the ears of those who were already seated in one. Nellie looked on helplessly, feeling her back pressed tightly against Henry, who sat behind her. Nellie's legs were pinned in place by the people to the front and sides of her. Nellie could not scream or cry or think—all she could do was stare at the scene of calamity aboard the Lusitania, which began sinking into the water.

People could be seen jumping off the side and pushing others off.

"There are enough lifeboats for everyone," Henry said in Nellie's ear, in an attempt to assure her that it was not as bad as it looked. He reached for Nellie's hand which lay limp at her side. Henry was worried that she had fallen unconscious and he twisted his body forward until he could see her face. Then Henry could see that she was still conscious, and was staring at something in utter fright. The woman with the baby still stood on the deck of the ship, and was extending her arms that held the baby over the rail, looking as if she would drop him into the sea.

The frightful scene went black as Nellie felt a warm hand cover her eyes. She could hear words being said into her ear, but she did not know what they were or what they meant. She did not feel like she was in her body, but rather high above the ship, watching the sinking from the sky.

"You're safe, you will see your family soon," Henry was saying. "You will be alright. We will reach land in no time. We are safe, and everything will be alright."

But he had spoken too soon. Before their lifeboat could be fully lowered into the water, it flipped to one side, sending its occupants in a free-fall into the sea. Nellie could feel herself falling through air, then falling through water, down, down, down. The cold water felt like needles pushing into her skin from all sides. She had no control over her body, tossing this way and that. The buoyancy of the lifebelt floated her to the surface where she gasped for air and swallowed water, gasping and choking at the same time. She watched in terror as the lifeboat sank, its former occupants scattered across the water.

"Nellie!" a voice echoed across the water, ringing in her ears as if it were only in her mind. "Nellie!"

She was able to turn her head enough to see Henry swimming toward her. Nellie's teeth were chattering and she did not speak as she remained in the stillness of shock. Her arms and legs were ice cold.

"There is another lifeboat just this way," Henry cried. "They have enough room for us if we hurry! Kick your legs behind you and follow me!"

Nellie obeyed as best she could, but her dress became heavy over her legs and Nellie was aware that kicking was doing no good at all. Henry pulled her through the water so that they could get closer to the new lifeboat. Debris from the ship along with floating bodies with vacant eyes surrounded them on all sides. Henry wished that he could spare Nellie the sight of the corpses, but was relegated only with telling her that they were almost to the lifeboat. By the time they finally reached the boat, it was clearly full.

"No more! We are full!" a man shouted from the boat. Henry looked on in dismay.

"It is Lord Caswell's son!" cried a woman's voice. "We have room for one more, surely!"

"I don't care whose son he is, if we get any more in here, we will go over!" another man argued.

"We cannot leave them here to die," shrieked a high woman's voice.

Henry spoke up from the water. "Here, take her!" he said about Nellie. "She will not weigh you down!"

Before anyone could argue, some people were already pulling Nellie into the boat. Others were looking across the way and screaming at the site of another lifeboat tipping when it tried to pull a person from the water. A man reached for Henry's hand and grabbed it tightly. "You better get on now before anyone notices!"

But Henry released the man's hand. He could see that the lifeboat was beyond capacity, and he was not going to be the one to send it into the sea. "Get to shore!" he demanded, swimming away and trying to stay afloat in the water. "Don't take anyone else on! Nellie, I will get on the next boat!"

The man who tried to help Henry gave him a mournful look. There were no other lifeboats near, and everyone knew it. Nellie could feel a dry jacket being placed around her shoulders as she sat shivering in her seat. The ladies were trying to comfort her with encouraging words. Nellie continued to shake with cold, watching the hundreds of lifeless bodies floating in the sea, and feeling as if she were one of them. One thing was certain to those who claimed the safety of the lifeboat—that the glorious Lusitania, their luxurious hotel for the last seven days, was now nowhere to be seen.

CHAPTER 6

There was a knock at the door of Lucy Whitmore's home in St. John's Wood. Julia answered promptly. "Good evening, Captain Perry," Julia said downcast, almost in a whisper.

"Then Lucy has heard the news," Captain Perry surmised.

Julia nodded. "Her ladyship is unable to receive visitors at this time."

"I understand, and I wish to help. Please tell her that I am here, Julia," he pleaded.

Julia allowed him to step into the entryway while she went upstairs to see her Mistress. Lucy was in her night-clothes in bed, holding a handkerchief to her face when Julia entered. "Captain Perry has come to see you, Madam."

"Frederick is here?" Lucy asked tearfully. "I cannot even stand up to greet him. My niece is almost certainly dead!" Julia nodded and returned downstairs to inform Captain Perry.

"Please, take me to her," Frederick insisted.

Julia looked aghast at the suggestion. "Her ladyship is beside herself with grief and remains in her bed. So you see, it would be impossible for you to see her now."

"It is a matter of life and death. I have come to be of

service, not to be entertained. Lucy need not leave her bed. Just take me to her."

Julia was hesitant but finally led him up the staircase. "I will go in first to tell her that you have come up," explained Julia. Frederick nodded. Then Julia exited the room and opened the door wide. "She is ready to see you."

Frederick walked into the dark room which was only lit by the glow from the fireplace. He could hear Lucy whimpering on the bed. He pulled up a chair to sit next to her. "I am terribly sorry, Lucy," he said.

"So am I," Lucy cried softly. "What a horrid thing to have happened to such an innocent girl!"

"Yes, it is horrid," Frederick agreed. "Have you heard—for certain—about your niece?"

Lucy shook her head. "I have not. I can only wait and hope to hear that she is soon on her way."

"I see," Frederick said. "I have come to offer my services. The rescue boats are running from Queenstown in Ireland. I will go there directly to look for your niece and her companion. When I find them, I will bring them here as soon as possible."

Lucy looked hopeful. "You would do this for us?"

"Of course I will. I do not wish to give false hope, but there are many survivors. Your niece may be one of them."

Lucy sniffled into her handkerchief. "We can only hope. But all of those poor people! The Germans are hideous for doing such evil!"

Frederick nodded. "We can talk about that later. For now, I must be leaving for Ireland. Do you have a photograph of your niece in case—in case I require it?"

"Yes, of course. Julia, please provide Captain Perry with Nellie's photograph," Lucy instructed.

Julia had been observing and listening from the doorway. "Yes, Madam."

"Her name is Penelope Whitmore, but she likes to be called 'Nellie'. She is twenty years of age, very fair, with light golden hair," Lucy explained.

"I will do what I can," Frederick promised, and was soon on his way to Queenstown with the photograph.

Rescue vessels reached the shores of Queenstown throughout the night. Henry Caswell was aboard one of them. There were many injured that Henry and the other able-bodied survivors attended to as best they could. When their rescue vessel pulled up to the harbor, the captain told them not to disembark until he had cleared it with the local authorities. Arguments broke out that some of the passengers needed medical attention and should not wait any longer to leave the boat, but the captain stood his ground. As soon as he was out of sight, the men on the ship tried to lower the gangplank so they could debark while a man on the dockside tried to stop them.

"You have three seconds to get out of the way," shouted one of the survivors. The men were able to finally lower the gangplank, and Henry and the others collected the injured to take them to the hospital. The lifeboats had not yet arrived in Queenstown. Henry hoped that Nellie was still in one of them.

The hospital was already full that night, with survivors being admitted with each new rescue boat. When Henry was walking out of the hospital, he brushed by one of the patients laid out on a cot and immediately felt a hand pulling on his arm. He turned around to see a woman with a bloodied shoulder lying down, looking frantically into his eyes. "Save me, Doctor!" she whispered hoarsely. Henry tried to ignore the chills that ran over his body, causing his hair to stand on end, and worked quickly to stop the bleeding from the woman's shoulder. After completing a bandage the best he could, one of the hospital staff spoke to him from behind. "Are you a doctor?"

"No," Henry replied. "But I want to stay and help, if it's alright."

"We need all the help we can get," the doctor answered gratefully. "You can clean and bind the wounds of those who are still arriving."

Henry set to work at the hospital, carefully overseeing the arrival of each new face throughout the night. Among those who came into the hospital, there was no sight of his aunt or uncle. At last he saw a familiar face, a pretty young girl with blonde hair whose hand he held that very afternoon. She was either asleep or unconscious, but to Henry's relief she was not injured. The hospital and hotels were filling quickly, and Nellie was carried away to a house nearby to stay overnight. Henry continued to help at the hospital, confident that his friend was in good hands.

When Nellie opened her eyes the next day, she looked around her in confusion. Everything about the room she lay in was unfamiliar. The room was dark and plain. There was nothing to decorate the walls, but Nellie was grateful for the warm fire which kept her from freezing. She recognized her dress and stockings hanging by the fireplace. She then looked down at herself and realized she was not wearing her own clothes.

"You're awake," said a woman's voice in a heavy Irish accent. "Want breakfast?"

Nellie turned her head groggily to see a woman sitting in a chair beside the bed. "Where am I?"

"Ireland," the woman responded. "The ship you came on was sunk by those Germans. Were you traveling with family, Dearie?"

"No…I was alone…" Nellie replied sleepily.

"Thank goodness for that. Hardly anyone survived. They've been pulling bodies from the sea all night."

Nellie felt her throat tighten up and tears fill her eyes. The woman looked at her sympathetically. "Oh I'm sorry, Dearie. I didn't mean to upset you. Sometimes I speak more than I should. What's your name?"

"Nellie Whitmore."

"Welcome to my home, Miss Whitmore. I dressed you in my daughter's clothes. You're about the same size, you see. Her dress is not so fine as yours. I've never seen clothes so fine in all my life. They are hanging there by the fire to dry, you see?"

"Thank you, Madam," Nellie told the woman.

The woman laughed. "I've never been called Madam in all my life. You must be delirious. Are ya hungry?"

"No, no thank you. But where is everyone from the ship?"

The woman shrugged. "Some here, some there. The hospitals and hotels are packed full. That's why they brought you here. No more room anywhere else."

"I must send word to my aunt in London that I am alright. She must be worried for me."

"But you'll be standing in line at the telegraph office all day," the woman said.

Nellie tried to sit up but suddenly felt the room rocking back and forth, just as the ship had felt on the sea. She was overcome with dizziness and closed her eyes.

"Don't try to get up now, Dearie. You can stay here for as long as you need, while you recover."

"Thank you," Nellie replied. She was going to say more, but was soon drifting back to sleep, dreaming that she was still aboard the Lusitania with Henry and Priscilla, as if nothing terrible had ever happened.

Captain Frederick Perry had driven through the night and boarded a ferry to reach Queenstown by the next afternoon. The city was a harrowing site as soldiers dug mass graves and forlorn passengers wandered the streets to identify their loved ones. Frederick felt his stomach sinking, but was determined to search for Nellie among the living before he searched among the dead. He went to the hospital and began to look over the people lying in makeshift cots and beds. Most of them appeared to be older than thirty years of age. After searching throughout the afternoon and inquiring of the staff with no progress, he turned to leave the hospital.

"Captain Perry?" said a voice from behind him. He turned to see who addressed him.

"Henry," he reacted in surprise. "I never expected to find you here. Were you aboard the Lusitania?"

"Yes, Captain," Henry answered. "As you can see, we had a dreadful time."

"Indeed," replied Frederick. "Have you been injured?"

"No, I have been helping with the wounded here. How long have you been in Queenstown?"

"I arrived just this afternoon. I am helping someone—a friend of mine—who had a relative aboard," Frederick explained.

Henry hung his head. "I hope you may return to your friend with good news, Captain. I am afraid that many did not survive."

Frederick nodded. "Were you traveling with family?"

"With my aunt and uncle. I have not seen them among the survivors, and it is presumed that all of the lifeboats have arrived by now."

"I am sorry, Henry. Truly. I wish you safe travels back to your family. I must continue on my search for this young lady," Frederick said, holding the photograph in his hand. "I don't suppose you have seen her here in the hospital? Penelope Whitmore is the name."

Henry felt his heart pound when he saw the photo. "Nellie," he said quietly. "She is not in the hospital, but you will be glad to hear that I have seen her alive with my own eyes. She was moved to a local house." He described to the captain how to get to the house where Nellie was taken.

Frederick breathed in relief. "Thank you, Henry. You have eased my search and my conscience. Her aunt will be overjoyed. Do you wish to ride back with us? Your mother and father must be sick with worry."

"I will stay to help until I am no longer needed," replied Henry. "Captain, will you see to it that my mother receives word of my well-being? They have already notified my father by telephone, but I would not wish for my mother to worry a minute longer than she already is."

"I will see to it, Henry. Goodbye."

Frederick arrived at the house that Henry told him about. An older lady answered the door. "Yes?"

"Good evening. I have been told that my friend's niece is staying here," he began, showing the photograph to the woman. "A Miss Whitmore."

"That's her, alright," the woman said. "Come in and sit while I fetch her." The woman disappeared down a dark hallway and Frederick waited in the sitting room.

Nellie was lying by the fire, watching the flames, when the woman walked into the small room. "A gentleman is here for you," the woman told Nellie. "Says he knows you."

Nellie held her breath and felt her heart race. She rose quickly and followed the woman to the sitting room, expecting to see Henry waiting there for her. Instead it was a man she had never seen before. She looked between the man and the woman in confusion.

"Good evening, Miss Whitmore. I am Captain Perry, here on behalf of your Aunt Lucinda."

"You know Aunt Lucy?" Nellie questioned.

"We are old friends," Frederick replied. "She gave me this photograph so that I may search for you among the survivors. Have you escaped without injury?"

Nellie did not know how to answer. Her mind was in a haze of confusion. Her eyes were injured by the sight of death, her heart injured by the pain of grief. "I am well in body, Captain," she finally replied.

"And…your traveling companion?" Frederick asked carefully.

Nellie realized that her aunt must have told him about Abigail. "My companion elected to stay behind in America."

"I see," Frederick replied. "Then I believe I should return you to your aunt without delay."

Nellie turned toward the woman. "Thank you for your kindness. I will change into my clothes now so I may leave with Captain Perry."

"Oh Dearie, your clothes won't be dry yet. There's so much material and so heavy. It will take another day or two by the fire."

Nellie nodded. "Might I borrow these clothes for now? I will post them to your house as soon as I am able."

"No need for all that," the woman replied. "The clothes are yours to keep. My daughter won't mind."

"Thank you, Madam," Nellie replied. "Perhaps your daughter would not mind keeping my dress in exchange."

The woman's eyes lit up. "Oh Dearie, she's never had anything so fine in all her life! It's not an even exchange. But if you insist…she'll be surprised when she comes home!"

Nellie smiled. It was the first time that she felt her face form a smile since she was last speaking with Henry. The smile felt foreign against her cheeks and a betrayal to her heart. She pushed dreadful thoughts to the back of her mind and replied to the woman. "Then it is settled. Thank you again." She then turned to Frederick. "Captain Perry, I am ready to go to my aunt's house now."

They took a ferry to the British mainland where Frederick had left his car, then began the long drive to London. Nellie did not say anything after they left the Irish woman's house, and Frederick did not expect her to. Nellie fell asleep in the car and did not wake again until they arrived at Lucy Whitmore's residence.

"Nellie! Oh, thank God you found her!" shrieked Lucy. "Come in, Nellie, Dear. Whose clothes are you wearing? Oh nevermind. I am so glad to you see you!"

Frederick led Nellie through the door. She walked slowly and stared blankly until she arrived to the guest room. She immediately lay on the bed and closed her eyes. Lucy looked at Frederick worriedly. "What is wrong with her? Was she injured?" she asked him.

"She has endured considerable grief," Frederick answered, shaking his head. "Queenstown was hell on earth. I am glad you did not have to see any of it."

"You did not find her companion?" Lucy whispered.

"Nellie said her companion stayed in America," Frederick replied.

"Thank Heavens," said Lucy. "I've been beside myself with worry. Were Nellie's suitcases recovered?"

Frederick shook his head. "It appeared the survivors only arrived with the clothes on their backs. I do not think anyone was concerned with suitcases."

"I see. No bother, I will have my dressmaker come first thing in the morning. Nellie will feel better when she has cheerful new clothes to wear."

Frederick sighed. "You should be careful with her, Lucy. The girl has been through a lot."

"Yes, of course. Thank you again for bringing her. I will see to it that she is well cared for," Lucy assured him.

"I am certain of that. Goodbye, Lucy." Frederick took his hat and left the house, anxious to return home for a good night's rest.

"We'll let her sleep as long as she likes tomorrow," Lucy said to Julia. "She should have breakfast taken to her room in the morning."

"Very good, Madam," Julia responded.

When the dressmaker arrived the next day, she took Nellie's measurements and reminded her not to slouch. Nellie did not realize that her shoulders were slumped forward or that it took great effort to stand straight with her head held high. She could still feel the sea under her legs. All she wanted to do was sit by the fire with a blanket wrapped around her body. Even while the room was warm, her teeth would chatter and shivers ran over her body. Lucy instructed the maids to be extra diligent about the fire in Nellie's room, and even worried that she may need to see a doctor. Nellie insisted that she did not need to see a doctor, and spent the days in her room.

Later in the week, Captain Perry came to the house with a list of survivors from the telegraph office. "I thought your niece might like to see this," he said to Lucy.

"I don't think it is wise. Will it only make her more upset?" Lucy questioned.

But Nellie was standing at the top of the stairs and heard their conversation. "Are those the names of the survivors?"

Lucy looked up to see Nellie standing there. "Yes, we were not sure if you wanted to see it."

Nellie hurried down the stairs, taking the list quickly and scanning the names as fast as she could read. There were no Campbells listed. Neither were there any Caswells. Tears fell down her face as she noted how short the list of names was.

"I did not intend to cause you distress, Miss Whitmore," Captain Perry said kindly. "I am sorry that the list is not longer."

"Wait a moment—my name isn't on here!" cried Nellie. "Why haven't they printed my name?"

"The list cannot be expected to be complete so soon," Frederick answered. "Your name may not be included because you were taken directly to a house instead of a hospital. There are surely other survivors who are not on the list, although it is not likely there are many."

"Then what good is this list anyway!" Nellie shouted, crumpling the paper in her hands and storming up the stairs. She could then be heard wailing from her room.

Lucy was aghast. "Captain Perry, I apologize! She is not usually like this!"

"I am not offended, Lucy. I only feel sympathy for the poor girl. She has undoubtedly lost friends from the voyage."

"Yes, you must be right," Lucy said thoughtfully. "The poor girl. I think I should go to comfort her now. Good day, Captain Perry." Lucy went up the stairs to Nellie's room, where Nellie lay crying on the bed. "I am terribly sorry, Dear."

"It's no use. They are all dead. The Caswells, Priscilla… Henry. It is my fault that Henry is dead. He could have gotten to safety, but he made them take me instead. It is my fault that he is drowned in the sea! I never want to hurt this much again! I won't love anyone again!" Nellie rambled incoherently through her sobs, the flood of memories pouring from where they were kept hidden in her heart.

Lucy looked on helplessly. She did not comprehend how bad it was until now. She brought Nellie a dry handkerchief and endless cups of tea as Nellie continued to relive the tragedy. "If there is anything I may do for you, all you need do is ask. I have already sent a telegram to your parents in Lancaster. They know you are safe here with me."

"We must inform Mary," Nellie said suddenly. "She must be crazy with worry. Will you send it to her, Aunt Lucy? I want all the girls at Davenport House to know that I am well. I almost brought them with me. I would have been to blame for their deaths too!"

"I will send the telegram right away," Lucy promised. "But Nellie, you are not responsible for anyone's death. It was those dreadful Germans who are to blame. You have done nothing wrong."

Nellie took a deep breath. "I should have forced Priscilla out of bed. She and the baby have drowned because I left her to sleep in the icy water!"

"You mustn't blame yourself," Lucy kept repeating.

Nellie continued to cry until tears would no longer come out. Exhausted, she leaned back onto her bed and fell asleep.

Henry Caswell was still at the hospital at Queenstown. He was discussing with Dr. O'Neil the possibility of an apprenticeship with him as a surgeon. He was not expecting his father to storm in just then.

"Henry!" growled his father. "What are you still doing here? Why haven't you returned home?"

"Father," Henry said in surprise. "I—I stayed to help with the wounded."

"You have no business here!. You are not a doctor! I demand that you come home with me at once! Your name is not on the survivors' list. Do you know what it has done to your mother to not find your name? Captain Perry came to call and told us you were alive and well, but your mother will not believe until she has seen you with her own eyes. Now come with me, before her heart fails her!" The Marquess spun on his heel and went out the door, expecting Henry to be right behind him.

Henry looked mournfully at the doctor. "I must leave now. Thank you for your advice, Doctor O'Neil. I hope to see you again soon."

"You are welcome anytime, Lord Henry. I wish you the best in your career."

Henry joined his father in the car that was waiting outside. "I am sorry, Father. I sent word with Captain Perry to ensure that Mother would not worry for me. I did not realize my name was missing from the list."

"Likely because you were pretending to be a doctor instead of thinking of your family," his father mumbled.

Henry bowed his head. "I am sorry about Uncle—"

"I do not wish to hear or speak of it," his father interrupted. "I only came for you to calm your mother's nerves."

Henry nodded, surmising that his father's anger was

coming from pain over the loss of his brother. Henry did not wish to upset him further, and responded submissively. "Yes, Father."

The next morning, Lucy and Julia were surprised when Nellie arrived at the breakfast table. "Good morning, Dear," Lucy greeted her.

"Good morning, Aunt," Nellie said quietly. "Please forgive my outburst in front of your friend yesterday. I know he was only trying to help."

"It is nothing to worry about," Lucy assured her. "Captain Perry was very understanding."

"He seems a good man. I am ashamed that I have likely appeared ungrateful to him thus far," Nellie cringed.

"At least you seem to be feeling better, Nellie," replied Lucy. "I was just telling my maid to send out announcements to cancel the party, in light of the circumstances."

"Oh, please do not cancel the party!" Nellie exclaimed.

Lucy raised her eyebrows. "But it is scheduled for Saturday. You cannot still wish to have the party…"

"I do," insisted Nellie, helping herself to a scone from the buffet. "I have already invited my friends from the voyage. I do not wish them to be disappointed if they are planning to attend. They were not on the list…but neither was I. Perhaps they have survived after all."

"Ah," Lucy said hesitantly. "Only if you are certain…"

"I am certain, Aunt. You need not worry on my account."

"Very well," Lucy acquiesced, nodding to Julia. "We will continue with the party on Saturday as planned."

Captain Frederick Perry visited on Friday with a bouquet of flowers for Nellie. Julia led him to the sitting room where he wait for Lucy. When she entered the sitting room, she gasped in delight to see the flowers. "How kind of you, Captain Perry," she greeted.

"Come now Lucy. You know you can call me Frederick. It is not as if I call you Baroness or Lady Whitmore," Frederick remarked.

Lucy gave him a look. "No, you certainly do not. The flowers are a nice gesture. I will have Julia set them in a vase."

"I brought them for your niece," Frederick said sheepishly. "To apologize for upsetting her the other day. Is she faring any better?"

"She is," replied Lucy, just as Nellie walked into the sitting room.

"Captain Perry," she greeted with a smile. Before Lucy could stop her, Nellie had gone across the room to give the captain a hug and kiss on the cheek. "I have never thanked you for your kindness, but please know that I am grateful for all you have done for me."

Frederick laughed. "I am glad to see you feeling better, Miss Whitmore. I brought these flowers to cheer you."

"How wonderful. Thank you," replied Nellie. Her spirits seemed high. Frederick and Lucy looked on in surprise. "You will come tomorrow, won't you?" Nellie asked Frederick.

"Of course I will," he answered slowly, looking between Nellie and Lucy.

"I am glad to hear it," Nellie replied. "If you will excuse me, I have a dress fitting I must attend. Goodbye." And with that, Nellie left the house.

"Am I invited to return tomorrow?" Frederick questioned, wondering if Nellie was confused.

"The party for Nellie," Lucy reminded him.

Frederick stared in disbelief. "I am astonished at you for not having canceled. After everything the girl has endured, how could you think such a thing is appropriate?" he asked in a scolding tone.

Lucy became defensive. "If you must know, I tried to cancel, but Nellie insisted that we carry on."

Frederick was quiet while he thought about it. "I am sorry, Lucy," he apologized. "I will attend tomorrow, if it is what you wish. I am only surprised, that's all." He paused before he continued. "When the invitation first arrived at my house, it was the most surprised that I have been in years."

Lucy looked down at her lap. "A good surprise, I hope?"

"Indeed." An awkward silence followed while Lucy thought of what to say next.

"I should be preparing for the party," she told him.

"Yes, of course. I will see you tomorrow. Goodbye, Lucy."

Lucy Whitmore's house had a grand ballroom that was polished from top to bottom and bursting with delight-ful flower arrangements. Lucy hired additional servants for the event to serve the food and drink. Nellie changed into her new gown for the party. She gazed at her reflection in the full-length mirror while her thoughts were miles away. "Please be here tonight," she whispered. The only way she managed to retain cheerfulness was by telling herself that her friends had survived, despite their names not being printed on the list. Nellie clung to the hope that Henry and Priscilla might walk through the ballroom doors at any moment. She could feel tears of doubt stinging behind her eyes, but she blinked them back, as she had done many times since the voyage.

Nellie slowly entered the ballroom filled with lords and ladies from around the country. The noise of their merry conversation echoed off the walls and sent Nellie back to the festive nights aboard the ship. She scanned over the faces in the crowd, longing for a familiar one that might ease her grief. Lucy prepared to make an announcement to the guests when Nellie walked in. "My lords, ladies, and gentlemen, may I present my niece, Miss Nellie Whitmore." Applause erupted from the guests, who had learned that Nellie survived the fateful voyage. Nellie forced a smile while Lucy came up alongside her. "Are you alright, Nellie?" she whispered.

"Of course," Nellie lied.

"The Duke of Staffordshire has asked to open the dance with you."

"Yes," Nellie responded distractedly. The music was soon playing and Nellie found herself in the center of the room with the handsome Duke. As the dance began, she could feel the guests staring at her while every whisper in the crowd sounded as if it was being said loudly in her ear. They whispered about torpedoes, war, bodies, and lifeboats. Nellie did not feel connected to her arms and legs that were dancing in time to the music. Captain Perry was watching her closely from the corner of the room.

When the first dance was over, the Duke remarked to Nellie, "You are a marvelous dancer, Miss Whitmore."

But Nellie was looking around the room frantically. "Can you tell me the time, Your Grace?" she asked abruptly.

The Duke removed his pocket watch. "It is half past the hour," he answered.

Nellie heard a voice from behind her. "Might I have the next dance?"

Nellie spun around. She searched the man's face for any degree of familiarity. Had she seen him before? She could not be sure. She saw his lips moving but she could not discern the words that were coming out. She looked again into the faces in the crowd. They began to blur together into faces that she had seen before, floating lifeless in the sea, their vacant eyes haunting her every thought. Nellie did not know that she had been holding her breath while the gentleman waited patiently for her answer about the next dance. Her heart was pounding loudly in her ears while her lungs tightened and burned. Her eyelids clamped shut and she was free falling again, waiting for her body to hit the icy water.

When Nellie opened her eyes, she was lying on her bed, and could hear voices arguing in the room. "I told Lucy she wasn't ready. How could she let this happen?"

"But Miss Nellie insisted, Captain. Her ladyship was only trying to make her happy," Julia's voice explained.

"Lucy may have good intentions, but you know very well that they do not lead to the best decisions," Captain Perry countered. "She can't have more parties like this. Not right now. Where is Lucy, anyway?"

"She is sending the guests home now, Captain," answered Julia. "I should be downstairs helping her."

"Go ahead and help her. I will stay with the girl," the Captain said.

"But—" Julia objected.

"It is fine. I will just be sitting in this chair until Lucy can get up here." After Julia left the room, Frederick noticed that Nellie's eyes were open. "You are awake. I am sorry about all that. Your aunt should be up here any minute."

"Is the party over already?"

"It is now. You need to rest," he answered.

"I don't remember coming to my room," Nellie thought aloud.

"You fainted after the first dance. The Duke helped carry you back to your bed."

"I had the strangest sensation that I was reliving that awful day," Nellie whispered.

"It is to be expected. There are things that will happen in life…reminders…that will bring the day so clearly to your mind as if it is happening all over again."

"How ever did you find me that day in Ireland? I have wondered how only a photograph could have led you to the woman's house."

"I was fortunate that day to see an acquaintance of mine—a young man who recognized you from the photograph. He told me where to find you."

Nellie jolted upright in her bed. "What young man?" she demanded.

Captain Perry was startled in his chair at Nellie's sudden reaction. "He is called Lord Henry Caswell."

Nellie's mouth hung open and her heart raced. "Henry is alive?" she cried.

"He was helping with the wounded at the hospital in Queenstown," Frederick answered. "I am sorry I did not think to tell you sooner. I assumed you knew."

"Of course I didn't know!" she shouted, leaping from her bed.

"Where do you think you are you going?"

"I'm going to Surrey. I need to see him with my own eyes."

"You cannot go now. You are not well," Frederick argued.

"I will be when I see him!" Nellie called as she hurried out the door.

"Please, Nellie, wait—" he called after her, following her down the stairs as quickly as he could. "At least tell your aunt—" But before he could finish, Nellie had left through the front door. When Frederick reached the door, he looked outside and could see no sign of her. He returned inside to find Lucy, who was busy with the guests remaining in the house. "I must speak with you Lucy," he said urgently.

Lucy politely excused herself and went with Frederick to the parlor. "My maid has already informed me that you are cross with me for having the party," she said. "If you are here to scold me, don't you think it can wait until after the guests have gone?"

"No, Lucy, and I am sorry for scolding you. I see now how persuasive your niece can be when she sets her mind to something."

"What do you mean?"

"She has gone."

"Gone where? Gone out of the house?" Lucy asked in disbelief.

"I tried to stop her, but she would not listen," he replied in embarrassment.

Lucy gasped. "We must find her! Where could she have gone?"

"I believe she is on her way to Caswell Castle in Surrey."

"Why in Heaven's name would she go there?" asked Lucy.

"I'll explain on the way, if you wish to go with me," Frederick offered.

"Yes, I'll just need to get my coat."

Henry Caswell dined with his mother and father in the grand dining room of Caswell Castle. An excess of footmen served the dinner while the family quietly ate at the table. Henry's father spoke suddenly. "None of this would have happened if you had married the American girl when you were supposed to. I've had no shortage of angry telegrams from the girl's family."

"I'm sorry, Father," Henry apologized. He had been

treading carefully around his father since he arrived home, knowing that he was grieving the loss of his brother, even if he did not show it.

"What are we supposed to do now? How can I hand the reigns of this legacy to a son who does not even care for it?"

Henry did not answer, but hung his head. His mother, the Marchioness, looked at him compassionately. "Are you recovered from the voyage, Henry?" she asked kindly.

"I am doing the best that I can," he replied vaguely, not wishing to worry his mother with the horrors he faced daily.

The butler suddenly spoke to Henry's father, the Marquess. "Forgive me, Your Lordship, but there is a lady at the front door who is asking to see Master Henry, urgently. I told her the family is at dinner, but she does not seem like she will leave."

Henry looked up quickly. "What lady?"

"She did not give her name. She is an American lady and appears to be quite distressed," the butler replied.

Henry scrambled out of his seat and ran from the dining room. His mother and father looked at each other. "What do you think that was about?" asked the Marchioness.

Her husband shrugged. "God only knows, with that boy."

Henry emerged through the doors leading to the castle entryway. Nellie stood there, trembling at the sight of him. "Nellie," he said gently, not knowing what else to say.

"I thought you had drowned, and that it was my fault," she whimpered.

Henry felt his heart beat faster as he moved close to her. "No, I didn't drown. And if I had, it would never have been your fault."

Nellie covered her face with her hands and wept into

them. Henry put his arms around her shivering body. She relaxed into the sudden warmth of his embrace, and did not think she could pull away from him if her life depended on it. She was able to explain herself better once she calmed down. "I did not see your name on the survivors list. I thought you were dead all this while. I knew you must be dead when I did not see you at the party tonight."

Henry was perplexed. "I am sorry you have worried about me all this while. If I had known you were still having the party, I would have come."

"Truly?" she asked.

"Of course. I have wanted to see you—I did not know if I should. I did not want to serve as a reminder for the dreadful events of that day."

Nellie looked up into his eyes. "But this is the happiest I have felt since that day."

"It is the happiest I have been, too," he confessed, his sorrowful eyes returning her gaze. "My parents are just upstairs. They will send a search party if I do not return and explain to them who was at the door. Wait here a moment, and I will return to speak with you properly. We can walk around the gardens, if you wish."

Nellie nodded and said, "I will wait for you."

Henry rushed back upstairs to the expectant faces of his mother and father. "Well?" his father coaxed.

"She is a lady I met on the voyage. She learned that I was a survivor and came to visit," Henry explained. "I have just offered to show her the gardens."

"At this time of the evening?" his mother questioned.

"The moon is full," Henry countered. "It is nearly daylight outside."

"Who is this woman, Henry?" persisted his father.

"She is called Miss Nellie Whitmore."

The Marquess was delighted at the response. "Miss Whitmore! And she wishes to see you? You must bring her up to meet us, Henry. Let her witness the splendor of our family dining room."

"Do you know of her?" the Marchioness questioned her husband.

"I know she is heiress to the fortune of the late Sir George Whitmore. My brother and his wife were meant to act as her chaperons during the voyage."

"Oh, I see," said Henry's mother. "Please do bring her up, Henry."

Henry turned and went back downstairs to see Nellie, who was drying her eyes. "I'm terribly sorry, but my parents are insisting that I bring you upstairs to meet them. I know it has been a difficult day—do not feel obligated, if you do not wish to." But it was too late. Henry's father had followed him down the stairs and was now standing next to Henry, waiting for an introduction. Henry sighed apologetically. "Miss Whitmore, this is my father, the Marquess of Caswell."

"How do you do, Miss Whitmore?"

"I am well, Lord Caswell. I hope that I may be forgiven for barging in tonight," replied Nellie.

"I did not realize that you and Henry were acquainted. You must visit him as often as you wish."

Henry glared at him. "Father…"

"Henry has said he will give you a tour of the gardens. The gardens have been laid for hundreds of years. They are as much a part of English history as Buckingham Palace," boasted the Marquess.

"I am certain to enjoy them, Lord Caswell," Nellie answered with a giggle.

"I'm sure you know that Caswell Castle is one of the last in England to have a functioning moat. But do not worry—the drawbridge is always let down," the Marquess continued with a wink.

Nellie smiled politely. She was pleased that Henry's father seemed eager to welcome her. But Henry did not seem comfortable during the conversation and was relieved to finally walk out the door with Nellie.

Frederick and Lucy had just arrived in the drive at Caswell Castle. Frederick parked the car and turned off the headlights just as Nellie and Henry emerged through the front door. "There she is," Frederick said. "It seems she is with Henry."

"But why would she come here now of all times?" Lucy asked.

"Can't you see? They have formed an attachment. It looks as if he is showing her the estate gardens. I remember doing the same at my family's estate when I was in love with a girl."

Lucy squirmed uncomfortably in her seat. "But I should go tell Nellie it is time to come home. She gave us a fright by leaving so suddenly. She must have hired a car to bring her here."

"Let them be, Lucy. It is clear that your niece has been anxious to see him. It would be cruel to pull her away so soon. Wouldn't you agree?"

Lucy sighed. "I will give them only a few minutes. Nellie knows better than to be alone with a man at night." Lucy could feel Frederick staring intently at her, but she sat up straight in her seat and refused to look back at him.

Nellie was not paying attention to the gardens as she and

Henry walked through the hedges. "Do you have nightmares about what happened?" she asked.

"I'm afraid I do every night. And sometimes, during the day," Henry admitted.

"What can be done about it?"

"I don't know that anything can be done about it. We must be grateful that our lives were saved and I suppose make the most of them."

"You saved my life," Nellie said quietly.

Henry smiled. "It may have been more selfish of me than it was heroic."

"How is saving the life of another ever selfish?" Nellie questioned.

But Henry changed the subject. "Thank you for coming to visit tonight. I wrote you a letter as soon as I returned home, but I have yet to send it. I can give it to you tonight."

"Why not just tell me what the letter says?" Nellie suggested.

"It is better if you read the words when you return to your aunt's house," Henry replied.

Lucy Whitmore continued to watch them from the distance and suddenly gasped. "He has just taken her hand! That's it, I must retrieve her now!"

Frederick laughed. "Is holding hands really so scandalous?" he asked.

Lucy huffed when she turned to him. "Nellie has a reputation to consider. I will not sit idly by and watch it be put to risk." Frederick was about to help Lucy out of the car, but she hurriedly climbed out on her own, her sudden rush causing her to trip to the ground. She fell on her face with a scream.

"Are you alright?" Frederick asked as he helped her off

the ground, stifling a smile. "Oh no, I am holding your hands. Do you think it will be printed in the newspapers tomorrow?"

Lucy glared at him while she pulled her hands out of his and wiped the dust off her dress. Nellie and Henry heard the noise and came over to investigate. "Aunt Lucy!" Nellie exclaimed. "What are you doing here?"

"I have come to take you home," Lucy answered. "Please get in the car so that we may put this night behind us."

"I will, Aunt, but please let me introduce my friend, Henry Caswell. He saved my life when our ship went down."

"Thank you, Lord Henry," Lucy said quickly.

"I am pleased to meet you, Madam," Henry replied. He took Nellie's hand again to help her into the backseat of the car. Then he discreetly pulled an envelope from his pocket and handed it to her. "Read this when you get home," he whispered.

"I will," she whispered back. She felt her hand brush against his one last time when she took the envelope. It sent a burst of electricity through her arm and shoulder, settling upon her racing heart. Judging by the look on Henry's face, Nellie was not the only one who felt something when their hands touched.

The drive back to London seemed tedious. Nellie apologized to her aunt for leaving the house so suddenly, but noticed that Lucy seemed to be bothered about other things that Nellie could not understand. She kept quiet for most of the drive.

When Nellie had said goodnight and was settled into her bedroom, she sat on the floor by the warm fireplace. She was nervous to read what might be in the envelope and she could not understand why Henry would not just tell her when they were in the gardens. Nellie slowly opened the letter and began to read. Tears stung her eyes and a lump formed in her throat. She covered her heart with her hand as the tears fell freely onto her lap, some landing on the letter and smearing the ink. She then lay on the floor and stared into the fireplace, slowly drifting into a peaceful sleep with the letter still in her hand.

Nellie,

I hope this letter finds you well. In our last moments on the Lusitania, you held a baby boy in your arms so that his mother could have a rest. I recall that the baby was taken with you as you held and smiled at him. But when we pulled away in the lifeboat, we watched the baby's desperate mother hold him over the side. I am writing to tell you that I have seen the boy and his mother, alive and well at the hospital in Queenstown. They survived with only bruises and scrapes. I even had the privilege of holding the boy through the night while his mother rested. You and I saw many terrible things that day, and we have many terrible memories as a result. I thought you should know that this does not need to be one of them.

Your friend,
Henry

Chapter 7

Nellie felt a renewed sense of strength when she arrived at the breakfast table the next morning. Lucy did not say another word about the previous night's events. She seemed to be preoccupied with thoughts of her own.

"How long have you known Captain Perry?" Nellie asked suddenly.

"What? Why should you ask such a thing?" Lucy answered defensively.

"When he introduced himself to me, he said that you were old friends. I just wondered how long you had known him. I never saw him before on my previous visits."

Lucy sighed. "No, I suppose you didn't. To answer your question, I have known the Captain for just over twenty years."

"Why, that is a lifetime," Nellie said in surprise. "He seems a nice man. Are you in love with him?"

"Nellie!" her aunt scolded. "Mind your tongue! You are going to give someone heart failure with your candid speech. Do not forget that you are not in America anymore, and such suggestions are most unwelcome."

Nellie bowed her head. "I'm sorry, Aunt. I do not even know why I said that."

Julia entered the room just then. "A gentleman caller is here for Miss Nellie," she announced. Nellie hurried to the washroom to check her appearance before Julia could say any more.

"Please show him into the sitting room, Julia," Lucy ordered. "I will be there in a moment."

Nellie practically skipped into the sitting room expecting to see Henry. "Oh. Good morning, Your Grace," she said to the Duke. Nellie seated herself in a chair and tried to mask her disappointment.

"Good morning, Miss Whitmore. I brought these flowers to cheer you. Your aunt has said that you are feeling better today," the Duke said politely.

"I heard that you carried me upstairs last night after my fainting spell. Thank you for your help.".

"It was my pleasure," he said with a smile. "I am glad to see you again, Nellie. I was worried that you had returned to America for good the last time."

Nellie shook her head. "I am not sure I wish to return now. I could never dream of boarding another ship across the sea!"

"No one could blame you for that," replied the Duke. "I understand that you are looking to marry."

Lucy looked up from her embroidery with wide eyes. She did not expect the Duke to be as blunt as her niece.

"My family wishes me to marry," answered Nellie. "And I suppose I must…someday."

The Duke laughed. "You amuse me, Nellie. I have always thought you had a spark of life in you that I do not often see in women. I think you would be a fun wife."

Lucy looked back and forth between the Duke and Nellie, hardly believing the conversation taking place.

"I am flattered, Your Grace. You have likely heard that I am the sole heiress of my family's fortune, but I think it only right to inform you that my mother is expecting another child. If she delivers a son, I will not inherit any fortune. So even if I was a fun wife, I would bring no money into a marriage with you."

The Duke laughed heartily. Lucy covered her heart with her hand and held her breath. "Nellie, honestly," she said nervously. "Give the Duke a chance to speak before you make such assumptions."

"She is right, Lady Whitmore. I have come to propose marriage. I do not care about the money. My family has more than enough to go around."

Lucy was nearly hyperventilating now. "Perhaps I will leave you two to speak," she told them. She gracefully left the room, leaving Nellie and the Duke alone.

"We have shocked her," Nellie giggled. "You are just as honest as I am, and Aunt Lucy can hardly tolerate when I speak plainly."

The Duke chuckled. "I prefer it this way. No reason to take years to say something that should only take minutes. Life is short, as I am sure you know."

"It is true," Nellie said thoughtfully.

"So what do you say to my proposal? We could have great fun traipsing across Europe for a honeymoon. I require a wife who will keep me entertained, and I know that you can more than anyone else."

"You offer everything that a lady could hope for, and I do not wish to appear ungrateful," Nellie said slowly. "But

I am afraid I cannot accept your proposal. You see, there is someone else."

"I see," the Duke said. "Then he is a lucky fellow. But if it does not work out with him, I hope you will consider me."

"Thank you, Your Grace. You will make a lady very happy someday. I am certain."

After the Duke left, Nellie was about to ascend the staircase to her room when Lucy stopped her. "Well?" she questioned anxiously. "Am I to congratulate you on your engagement? Are you to be the next Duchess of Staffordshire?"

Nellie sighed. "I declined his proposal, Aunt."

Lucy's mouth hung open. "What possible reason could you have to decline him? Even when you admitted you might be left penniless, he still wished to marry you. You cannot be picky anymore, Nellie. I only hope that you reconsider and that the Duke is still willing to take you after you have insulted him."

"Post for Miss Nellie," Julia announced, holding a platter with a letter.

Nellie was grateful for the interruption and quickly read the letter. "It is from Caswell Castle. The Marquess has invited me to dine tonight," she told her aunt, expecting to see a reaction of approval. Lucy, however, did not seem pleased, and turned to leave the room.

Nellie wore a new evening gown to the castle that night. Henry's father immediately gave Nellie a tour of the castle until Nellie's legs were tired from walking. "It has been in my family for hundreds of years," the Marquess was saying. "Of course, we wish it to be preserved for hundreds more."

"It is a marvelous home," Nellie agreed. Henry walked alongside them during the tour but did not say much. Even at dinner, he seemed quiet and only forced a smile when Nellie would look at him. Nellie observed that the number of footmen and other servants seemed as many as might be at the palace of the king and queen. The dinner that night included rare and exotic delicacies. Nellie could not help but be impressed by the opulence of their lifestyle, especially when Henry seemed so down-to-earth.

After dinner, Nellie went into a drawing room with the Marchioness, as it was customary for the ladies to exit the dining room before the men. "My son tells me that you became good friends on the voyage," Henry's mother said kindly.

"We did. I was abandoned by my traveling companion just as we boarded the ship in New York. But now after everything that has happened, it is a great relief to know that she stayed safely behind," Nellie explained. "Henry—um, that is—Lord Henry—was marvelous for conversation over the voyage. Did he tell you that he saved my life when our ship went down?"

The Marchioness smiled warmly. "He is too modest to admit such things. It does sound like my Henry, though. I am glad you told me."

While Nellie and the Marchioness spoke in the drawing room, Henry and his father remained in the dining room. The Marquess was insistent. "You must act now, Henry. It is all over town that the Duke of Staffordshire wishes to claim her for a wife. Ask her tonight before she accepts him and you lose her forever."

"If she wishes to marry the Duke, then who am I to prevent her? It is her decision, not the Duke's, or yours, or anyone else's."

The Marquess was aghast. "Do you mean to say you will not ask her tonight? And leave our family's legacy to crumble when I am dead? It is your duty to your family!"

Henry sighed. "I want to ask her, Father. But not like this." He suddenly rose from his chair and left to join the ladies in the drawing room.

"Henry," Nellie greeted with a twinkle in her eye. "Your mother was just telling me marvelous things about you."

Henry laughed nervously. "I am certain she was. Nellie, what do you say to a tour of the dungeons? I know you were disappointed to not be able to see them before."

"Oh," Nellie giggled. "I would be glad to, now that the wonderful dinner has given me my strength back."

Henry brought a large candlestick to light the way on the tour. As they descended the dark stairwell, he paused to light the candles along the walls. The light from the flames danced in the otherwise dark dungeons. Nellie smiled. "I forgot how romantic it can be to light the way by candlelight. Modern lights do not have the same effect."

"My father hopes to install electric lights in the near future. We do have a telephone, at least," he said.

"But Henry, why do you not seem happy to see me?" Nellie asked abruptly.

Henry chuckled at her bluntness while he set the candlestick on a table. "On the contrary, I am always happy to see you."

She raised her eyebrow at him. "Are you certain about that? You barely looked at me during dinner."

Henry sighed. "I know there is no fooling you when I am upset. Do you remember my story of being sent to America to marry that girl?"

"Of course I remember," Nellie replied. "You said that she was kind and beautiful, but you refused her."

Henry cringed. "Yes, well, you see—it has happened again. My father is pressuring me to marry a girl for her money. Except this time, I have already met the girl—and I understand now what people mean when they say they have fallen in love."

"I think I understand it too," Nellie said, facing him. "And are you going to refuse this girl as you did the last one?"

Henry looked into her eyes intently. "That is the last thing I want to do. But Nellie—my family is bankrupt. The dinner you attended tonight—it was all for show. My father can barely pay the servants their wages. He wants to use your fortune to sustain this castle, which grows more expensive to maintain by the day."

Nellie looked down at the floor. "I see. And this is why he and your mother have welcomed me so kindly."

"My mother can always be relied upon to be kind. It is my father whose actions toward you have been with motive," Henry clarified.

"You have told me the truth about your family's circumstances, and now I must tell you mine. In a few short months, I will no longer be the heiress to my family's fortune. My mother is expecting a child. The fortune will be divided if it is a girl, and if it is a boy, I will have nothing. It is why they sent me here to Britain, so that I could be married while I was still an heiress." Nellie looked at the floor in shame.

A look of realization crossed Henry's face and he gently lifted Nellie's chin so he could look into her eyes again. "This is perfect," he whispered.

"How is it perfect? I have nothing to offer your family.

Your father will not be so keen on a marriage between us when he understands my circumstances."

"I don't care about that, Nellie. I want to marry you, and I need you to know that it is because I love you and not your money."

"You love me?" Nellie asked, wishing to feel the pleasure of hearing the words again.

"I love you more than anything," he replied. They stood there for a moment, quietly looking at each other. Finally Henry said, "Would you do me the honor of becoming my wife?"

"Yes, I would like that very much," she smiled. Then she laughed. "I cannot believe I have become engaged in a dungeon."

Henry laughed too. "Has anything been normal since the day I met you? I suppose it is a sign that our lives together will never be predictable."

"But Henry, you must tell you father the truth about me. We could not begin our lives together by misleading your family," Nellie insisted.

"You are right. I will tell him now and get it over with. But first," Henry said, wrapping his arms around her. "I want to hold you for as long as I can, until they come looking for us."

Nellie sighed dreamily when she felt the warmth of his arms holding her tightly. "I agree, this is far better than telling them now."

At Lucy Whitmore's home in London, Captain Perry had been invited for tea in the drawing room. "To what do I owe this honor?" Frederick asked mischievously when he entered the drawing room.

"I never said thank you for helping with Nellie last night," Lucy answered. "I may not always agree with you, but I still must thank you for all you have done."

"It was my pleasure, Lucy. And how is she today?"

"She is not here. She is dining at Caswell Castle tonight," Lucy said, wrinkling her nose.

"What is wrong with that?"

"The Duke of Staffordshire paid Nellie a visit this morning. He proposed to her, and she refused. I hope that she reconsiders. He has taken the news of her dwindling fortune with perfect grace."

"But what about Henry? I have known him for years, and I can tell you he is a splendid lad. Nellie would gain a title by the marriage…which as I recall is rather important to you," Frederick answered with a hint of resentment.

Lucy looked down at her teacup in her hand. "Indeed, he is the son of a Marquess. But Nellie's father does not care so much for titles."

"Then why be in favor of the Duke over Henry?"

Lucy was sure that her answer would not go over well with Frederick. She stayed quiet until the silence became unbearable. "Everyone knows that the Caswells have been bankrupt for years," she finally blurted.

Frederick sighed exasperated and leaned back in his chair. "Don't you wish the girl to be happy? You know that they have already formed an attachment. Marriage to the Duke would only be for practicality. Can you truly say that you were happy in the practical sort of marriage you are now pushing onto her?"

Lucy glared at him, knowing that it is what Frederick had wanted to say all along. "This is not about me. I promised Nellie's father, and I must keep my word."

Frederick breathed angrily through his nostrils. "When did this conviction start?" he questioned, making no attempt to disguise his bitterness. "Lucy, do you realize that everyone heard about your dear Sir George being jilted by a rich American girl, and that he only wished to make a fast marriage with you? But you never meant a thing to him, you were only there for the sake of convenience. Is that what you want for your niece? To be a thing of convenience or amusement, instead of a lady who will be loved properly? Or do you wish for her to be as miserable as you, living with a man who—"

"Enough! Stop!" Lucy demanded. "It is not proper to speak of the dead—especially when the dead you speak of is my own husband! Leave now, Frederick. I will not hear another word from you." Lucy stood hastily and left the room.

Frederick was well aware that he had gone too far. He hated himself for letting the cruel words escape his lips, causing Lucy pain that she did not deserve. With his head bowed in shame, he left the house as Lucy had asked. He was sure that he would not be invited back.

At Caswell Castle, Henry spoke to his father in the study while Nellie waited patiently in the hallway. When Henry emerged through the doors and closed them behind him, Nellie could tell that something was wrong. "What did your father say?" she asked.

"Let us go into the library where we can speak privately," Henry answered solemnly. They settled into the library and closed the doors. "As can be expected, my father did not take the news well. He said the dowry is not adequate. He will only allow the marriage to take place if you are able to keep half your fortune."

"But I will not know until after the baby is born," Nellie objected. "But Henry, what if the baby is a boy? Would that mean that you will not marry me at all?"

"I would marry you today if I could. But as long as

I am under twenty-one, my father has the right to forbid our marriage."

"How can he do so?" asked Nellie.

"He said that unless you keep half your inheritance, he will forbid the reading of our marriage banns at every church. If the marriage banns are not read, we cannot be legally married."

"What if we wait until you are twenty-one?" she questioned.

"We could," Henry said mournfully. "If you are willing to wait another year. There are rumors that the Duke of Staffordshire is eager to make you an offer."

"He did just this morning," Nellie admitted. "Even after I told him that I will lose my fortune, he said he wished to marry me."

"I see." Henry swallowed the lump in his throat. "I have nothing to give you, Nellie. You might consider his offer."

Nellie looked painfully into Henry's eyes. "I want to be with you. I will wait until your birthday if there is no other way."

Henry could feel his heart leap in his chest and he repressed the urge to convince Nellie that she deserved better than him. "There is another way," he said slowly. "We can go to Scotland. It does not have the same marriage restrictions as we do here, and many go there to marry in a town just past the English border. It is called Gretna Green."

Nellie's eyes widened. "I have heard of Gretna Green. But isn't it rather scandalous to be married there?"

"Yes," Henry confessed. "I never understood before why anyone would wish to…but I understand now."

"My Aunt Lucy is the only family that I have here," Nellie said thoughtfully. "If I fall out of her good graces, I will have no one. And you will surely be out of the good graces of your own family."

"It is true," Henry said, his eyes sorrowful once more.

"I should be returning to my aunt's house now," Nellie told him.

Henry took her hands in his and became serious. "I know that I have put you in an impossible engagement. Any man would be fortunate to have you for a wife, and I won't expect you to marry me when you have a better offer. No one could blame you for marrying the Duke—not even me."

Nellie was not considering his words. Before she knew what she was doing, she had leaned into him and was pressing her lips against his. Henry forgot about any objections he had and passionately kissed her back, holding her tightly in the way he had wanted to since the first day on the ship. After a few minutes of kissing her, Henry pulled away reluctantly. "This is making it very difficult to say goodbye to you, Nellie. Your aunt will be worried."

Nellie was smiling. "Don't worry. When I get back, I will persuade her that I should marry you. I can be very persuasive, you know."

"I don't doubt it for an instant," he said smiling. The library doors opened just then and the butler came through.

"The car is still waiting for Miss Whitmore," he announced impatiently.

Henry walked with Nellie out of the castle under the watchful eyes of the servants. After he helped Nellie into the car, she looked at him intently. "Henry? There is one more thing I must tell you."

"Yes?" he responded.

"Thank you for the letter," she said. Henry squeezed her hand and watched emotionally as she drove away in the car.

Nellie arrived at her aunt's house and went straight to her bedroom. Lucy knocked on the door shortly after she heard Nellie come into the house. "Good evening, Dear. Look what the Duke has sent over for you! They are chocolates from Switzerland. Was not that generous of him?"

"His Grace is very kind," Nellie answered.

"I don't suppose you have reconsidered…" Lucy trailed off.

"It is no use, Aunt. I am in love with Henry Caswell."

Lucy put her hand over her heart. "How do you know you are in love with him?"

"I kissed him tonight and it was the most magnificent feeling on earth," Nellie sighed.

Lucy gasped. "Did you not have a chaperon at dinner?"

Nellie skipped past the question. "I have accepted his offer of marriage. I only hope that you can be happy for me."

Lucy appeared pale. "I promised your father that I would make a suitable match for you. What will he think?"

Nellie's face fell and she felt her teeth clenching. "My father sent me into a sea of u-boats when the whole world is at war. I don't care a smidge what he thinks right now."

"Nellie, that is not fair. Your father loves you very much and certainly would not have sent you if he knew," Lucy countered.

Nellie responded emotionally. "How can you be on his side? He does not care if he ruins me! He is happy to leave me with nothing so long as he gets the son he has always wanted. I have been a disappointment to him since the day I was born. It is because of him that I have been put in this position!" Lucy did not have an argument and stared blankly. "I am sorry, Aunt. I know that none of this is your fault and that you only want what is best for me. It is difficult for me to care what my father thinks right now. It is your opinion that I value—and I do not want to disappoint you."

"Does the Marquess know that you may lose your fortune?"

Nellie nodded.

"And what does he say about it?" Lucy questioned.

"He is opposed to the marriage unless I keep half my inheritance. He will forbid the reading of our marriage banns otherwise."

"Then it won't be possible for you to marry anyway," Lucy remarked.

"It will be possible if we go to Scotland," Nellie said quietly.

Lucy gasped again. "Good Heavens! You were raised better than this, Nellie! Please, give yourself time to think about what you are saying. You have been through so much this week, and it is causing you to make drastic decisions!"

Nellie felt tears forming. "Aunt Lucy, don't you remember what it is like to be in love?"

Lucy felt her heart ache while she held back her own tears. "It was a very long time ago," she whispered, standing up to leave the room. "You should rest now. It has been a long day."

As she slept that night, Nellie dreamed that she was aboard the Lusitania again, scrambling into the lifeboat when the ship started to sink. But this time, Henry was not in the lifeboat with her. It was too late to get back onto the ship to look for him. Nellie cried his name, but he was nowhere to be seen by the time the men lowered the boat into the water. Nellie looked at the other people in the lifeboat with her. They all had vacant stares, their lifeless bodies lying in the boat while Nellie stood up screaming for help. The boat rocked as if it would tip over. Then she saw Henry, still on the ship, sinking with it through the water.

"Nellie!" cried Lucy, attempting to shake her niece awake in the bed.

Nellie sat up straight in bed, staring in fright at nothing. "Henry!" she cried, reaching out and grasping the air in front of her.

"It is only a nightmare," Lucy told her. "You are safe in London now."

"But Henry is dead! And it is my fault!" Nellie cried, not fully awake.

"It is a bad dream. Henry is well and you have seen him just today, Dear."

"Did I?" Nellie said in confusion. Then she lay back down and fell asleep. Lucy went out the door and saw Julia waiting in the hallway.

"Is Miss Nellie alright, Madam?"

"She had another nightmare," Lucy explained. "The poor girl. I wish there was something I could do for her."

"Perhaps Captain Perry can speak with her," Julia suggested.

"What do you mean? Why him, of all people?" Lucy snapped.

"Forgive me, Madam. I only mentioned it because he is a sea captain and has experience with such matters," Julia answered.

"Oh. Yes, I suppose he is. But I do not want to ask Captain Perry to return to the house. I am going back to bed now."

Julia's eyes were wide when she replied, "Yes, Madam."

Nellie arrived at the breakfast table the next morning looking subdued. Her shoulders slumped and she could not manage a smile, even for Julia. Lucy looked at her in concern. "Is there anything I can do for you, Nellie?" Nellie shook her head and looked down at her plate. The breakfast did not appeal to her, even though it was the same as it was yesterday when Nellie had enjoyed it.

"The Duke of Staffordshire has come to call," Julia announced.

"Thank you, Julia," Lucy said. She whispered across the table to Nellie, "You do not need to seem him if you do not wish to."

Nellie looked sorrowfully at her aunt. "Thank you, Aunt Lucy." She rose from her seat and returned upstairs to her bedroom, leaving the untouched plate of food on the table.

Lucy met the Duke in the parlor and thanked him for his gifts, but explained that Nellie was not ready for visitors. He understood and left the house with a courteous smile. Julia met Lucy in the parlor after his departure.

"Your Ladyship, there is something I must tell you," she began nervously.

"Go on," Lucy replied.

"You might be cross with me for telling you this now, but Captain Perry has written you a letter that I have kept from you."

Lucy opened her mouth indignantly. "Julia! I cannot believe you could do such a thing! Why would you keep the post from me? When was this letter received?"

"It was twenty-three years ago, Madam," Julia answered sadly. "It was when—when you were in your room." Lucy clutched her chest and immediately sat down on a chair. She could not speak and was not sure if she could breathe. Julia continued, "Your parents insisted that I put the letter into the fire when they saw that it was from…him. I told your parents that I destroyed it, but…" Julia removed an envelope from her apron pocket and held it out to Lucy.

"I can't," Lucy said breathlessly. "I will faint if I read it now."

Julia nodded and placed it gently on the end table. "Forgive me, Madam."

Lucy took the letter upstairs to her room and locked the door. She sat on the bed and shook her head in anguish when she began to read. Tears fell down her cheeks with each word, and as painful as it was, she read the letter over and over again, until she fell asleep.

Lucy,

My Dearest Love, what have I done to deserve this punishment? I waited in Gretna Green as we agreed. It rained so terribly that I was frozen to the bone. But far worse than that, I suffered when I thought of what must have happened to you on the way. Your carriage must have overturned, or some terrible illness must have taken you. I waited the hours in anguish thinking you must be dead, and that it was my fault for insisting we travel separately. I watched every bend in the road on my return hoping to find you. I mourned with each village I passed where there was no sign of your travel. It was only when I returned home that I heard you were still at your parents' home…but that you had become engaged to a baronet! I feel like the rain never stopped. Every day I am chilled to the bone to think of what I have lost. I must have done something dreadful, only I do not know what it is. How is it that you told me you loved me one day, and promised yourself to another man the next? Whatever it is, let me beg your forgiveness before you marry him, so that our love may have another chance. I await your reply in the deepest agony that is possible for a man to endure.

Yours Forever,
Frederick

Chapter 8

"Captain Perry is here to see you, Your Ladyship," Julia announced.

Lucy took a deep breath before meeting him in the drawing room. Frederick stood up when Lucy entered, but his expression was grave. "Good afternoon," he said, barely above a whisper. "I have brought this survivors list from the telegraph office. It is longer than last time, and I was not sure if your niece would like to see it. I will leave it here with you in case she does."

"Thank you, Captain Perry. If you'll excuse me, I will take it to her now. Please wait here, for I have more to say to you."

Frederick nodded slowly and sat down on the settee. Lucy took the list up to Nellie's bedroom where Nellie had spent the past several days. "Captain Perry has brought you an updated survivors list," Lucy said gently.

Nellie scanned it quickly. "May I use the telephone?" she asked.

"Of course, Nellie. Julia will show you where it is," Lucy answered. She then returned to Frederick in the drawing room. "I owe you an apology," she began, slowly lowering herself into a chair.

Frederick looked at her in surprise. "It is I who should apologize to you, Lucy. I never should have said those things about your husband. It was thoughtless of me. Please, forgive me."

Lucy could not look him in the eye. "You were right when you said that George never cared for me. Some women have no children because nature will not allow them the chance. But I am without children because I never had the chance from my own husband. I do not need to be reminded of this humiliation that I live with every day."

Frederick felt his heart sink into his stomach while Lucy spoke of her pain. He could not say a word, only remained there sorrowfully.

Nellie walked into the doorway of the drawing room just then. She was wearing her hat and coat and carrying a traveling case. "Where are you going, Nellie?" asked Lucy, although she could guess the answer.

"Forgive me, Aunt. I am going to Scotland. I have just called Henry and we have it arranged. I cannot wait any longer. Life is so very short and I did not realize how short until the voyage. No one on the ship could have known that they would die that terrible day, and I can only wonder what they might have done differently if only they knew how little time they had left. I do not know how much time I have left, but I know I want to spend it with Henry."

Lucy gave Frederick a helpless look. He looked back at her with tears in his eyes. Lucy turned again to Nellie. "Please wait a moment while I get my coat. I will order the car and take you to Scotland myself. I want to be sure you get there safely."

Nellie breathed in relief. "Thank you, Aunt," she whispered emotionally. When Lucy returned with her coat, she told Nellie to wait in the car while she said goodbye to Captain Perry.

"Frederick, I am sorry I cannot finish our conversation now," she apologized, holding out a paper for him. "I wrote this for you last night in reply to your letter."

"My letter?" he asked bewildered.

"Yes, and I am sorry it has taken so long for me to write back," she answered. She quickly kissed his cheek and left through the front door. Lucy and Nellie were soon on their way to Gretna Green together.

In the east wing of Caswell Castle, Henry softly knocked on the door of his mother's bedroom. "Mother," he said when he opened the door. "I have to leave for a while."

His mother smiled at him. "I know."

"You do?"

His mother nodded. "I want you to give her this," she said, taking a jeweled ring from her finger.

Henry looked at her in astonishment. "Are you certain?"

"Yes," she said peacefully. "It was a gift to your grandmother from Queen Victoria. I wish for it to always be kept in the family. And do not worry about your father. I will see to it that he receives Nellie as kindly as she deserves."

"Thank you, Mother," Henry said, overcome with emotion. "While I am away, will you tell Father something for me?"

"Of course, Henry."

"On the last night that I saw my uncle, he said that he wished to come here to the estate. He expressed that he wanted to go fishing with Father once again. I have not known how to say it without upsetting him."

"It is something your father desperately needs to hear,"

Henry's mother replied. "Now go, Henry. You mustn't keep your bride waiting."

Captain Frederick Perry returned to his home, his heart pounding each time he thought of what the letter from Lucy might say. He waited until he was alone in his study to open it and begin reading.

Frederick,

I was shocked and dismayed to discover that you had written me a letter twenty-three years ago that I never knew existed until now. My maid has just shown it to me, and explained that my parents told her to destroy it when they saw that the post was from you. This is my long overdue reply.

On that day, I had packed my bags and was ready to meet you as I promised. My parents were not meant to be home then, but they arrived early, just in time to discover me preparing for the journey to Gretna Green. They locked me in my room for days and would only let me out on two conditions—that I marry Sir George Whitmore who had just returned from America, and that I never speak to you again. I was reluctant and anguished when I agreed to their terms. I did not know what other choice or escape I had, for if you'll recall, my bedroom was on the third floor of the house. I hoped that in the years since, you would forget about me and find happiness in life.

I would have met you in Scotland if it were possible. I often think of how different life would be if only I had left a few moments earlier. Please do not hate me for what happened in those days. It was never my choice to marry anyone other than you.

Lucy

PART II

Much had happened at Davenport House while Nellie was away. Abigail was married to the stable boy, Ethan. Clara Davenport was named as the sole heiress to Davenport House, and Mary discovered that her true father was John Smith, groundskeeper of the estate. Mary, along with her brother Ethan, came into the inheritance of a grand manor house in Philadelphia. Their father married again and was on his way to the train station with his new bride, when Dr. William Hamilton stopped him to ask a question…

Chapter 9

"John!" William called breathlessly as he hurried to the car, hoping to catch John Smith before he drove away.

"Thanks for coming today," John replied. He reached out to shake William's hand.

"Oh, of course, John, I mean, Sir—" William sputtered. "I have come to ask you something. It's about Mary."

John laughed. "I was wonderin' when you were going to say something. Nothing like waiting 'til the last minute."

William smiled sheepishly. "I'm sorry—so much has happened and—"

"No need to explain," chuckled John. "I've known you since you were a boy, and there is no other man that I'd wish for Mary."

William began to get choked up. "Thank you, Sir," he said. "Then—we may have your blessing?"

John nodded solemnly and gave him another handshake. "Take good care of her, William. She has been through much suffering, and it's high time she should be happy again."

Mary Davenport said her goodbyes to the newlyweds

just as she noticed that a messenger was leaving the house. She went inside to see Fiona, the housekeeper, waiting in the Hall. Fiona looked up at Mary. "A telegram has arrived for you, Miss," she announced.

"Thank you, Fiona." Mary's eyes grew wide and she called out. "Clara, come see! I believe it is from Nellie in London!" Clara Davenport was on the staircase just then and hurried over to read the telegram with Mary.

MISS MARY DAVENPORT
DAVENPORT HOUSE, YORK COUNTY, PENNSYLVANIA

MARY WHAT DO YOU THINK STOP I HAVE MARRIED LORD HENRY CASWELL AND WILL LIVE IN A GRAND CASTLE STOP IT MUST SEEM QUICK TO YOU BUT I HAVE LEARNED THAT LIFE IS TOO SHORT TO WAIT STOP

LADY NELLIE CASWELL

Mary and Clara giggled in delight, and did not notice when William had walked into the house. "Can you believe it?" exclaimed Mary. "Nellie, married already! I wonder what sort of man could have convinced her that she wanted to be a wife?"

Clara laughed. "Clearly a British Lord who lives in a castle, as is every girl's dream."

"Indeed. Nellie has found her Prince Charming, and I am glad for her," Mary smiled. She noticed William standing in the room just then. "William, did you hear? Nellie has been married!"

William chuckled nervously. "I did hear. I am glad she found happiness after the terrible ordeal with the ship."

"I will find Abigail and tell her the news," Clara stated, just before she hurried off to find her. William and Mary were alone in the great Hall of the house.

"May I speak with you now, Mary?" William asked.

Mary's eyes lit up when she remembered their prior conversation about William wishing to speak to her father. "Oh! Yes, of course!" She led William up the grand staircase and they settled into the upstairs sitting room. Mary looked at William expectantly as he closed the double doors behind him. He sat next to her on the settee and took her hands in his.

He began to speak quietly. "I want to marry you. John has given his blessing for me to ask for your hand. I do not feel adequate to ask you the question I have wanted to ask for a long time, so if it does not suit you, you can tell me now before—"

"I want to marry you too," Mary interrupted. "You only need ask."

William reached his arms around her, holding her and resting his chin on her shoulder. "Will you be my wife?" he asked.

"Yes," she quickly answered. Mary was smiling when she could feel his arms holding her tighter. "I love you more than anything. How could you ever feel inadequate?"

William sighed, pulling away from her. "When you and Clara were downstairs, you agreed that marrying a man of title to live in a castle was every girl's dream. I suddenly became worried, because I have no title or money, and my occupation is demanding. I only hope that you can be happy being the wife of a poor doctor."

"I am not worried about any of those things," Mary assured him. "My aunt has been generous and I will be careful with the money she has left me. We will be fine."

"And you realize that my job is demanding at times—and upsetting—and that there are things about my job that I will not be able to tell you," he continued.

"Of course I realize that," replied Mary. "I feel sorry for you and all the ghastly things you must witness at the clinic. I am grateful that I am not told the details."

William smiled. "I love you dearly, Mary," he said, and leaned in to kiss her. Just before their lips met, he whispered, "I cannot wait to be married to you."

At the Davenport's stable, Ethan was setting up the carriage with his horses. He and Abigail were leaving for Philadelphia to see the manor house he gained as an inheritance. "You will love the house," he was telling Abigail. "It is even grander than this one, if you can believe it."

Abigail was beaming. "I am glad to finally see it! And I am glad that we can be alone together for awhile."

Ethan smiled at her. "We cannot be gone for more than a couple days. I asked Phillip to look after the house and Mary's horse while we are gone, but there is much to be done on the grounds now that Pa has left."

"Has Mrs. Price sent inquiries for a new groundskeeper?" questioned Abigail.

"She told me that she is interviewing someone today. I only hope the man is good enough to get the job done," Ethan answered.

Abigail laughed. "You will not think anyone is good enough after your pa has been doing the job all these years."

"You're right about that," he replied. "Pa was the best, and he always will be."

After William left Davenport House to return to the clinic, Mary met Clara in the drawing room. Clara was embroidering a new pillow and looked up from her stitching.

"Why, you look flushed, Mary! What have you and William been up to?"

Mary grinned as she told her the news. "We are engaged."

Clara gasped. "Oh my goodness! This means there will be another wedding! Do you wish to marry here at the house? You will make the most darling bride. I cannot wait to get started!"

Mary laughed. "I have not figured any of that out yet. The engagement has only just happened! But I assure you that I will depend on you in the coming weeks to help me with the planning. I don't know a thing about weddings!"

Clara stood up from her seat and clasped her hands together in delight. "Oh this is the happiest moment of my life! My best friend in all the world getting married! I must tell Mother right away. And my Aunt Catherine! Did you know that she is moving upstairs today?"

"How wonderful," Mary answered. "Your aunt will enjoy being served for once, I am sure."

Clara hugged Mary and kissed her on the cheek, then sighed almost as if she was sorrowful. "I am getting too old to ever be wed. I suppose I will have nothing better to do than plan the weddings of my friends."

"You are only twenty-five," Mary said, even though she knew it was considered old for a bride. "And you are beautiful, kind, and rich. If you wish to get married, there is nothing to stop you."

"Except for not having a single suitor," Clara laughed. "I hope I may find a man as good as your William. He is everything a girl could hope for in kindness."

"It is why I love him so terribly," Mary smiled. "Where is your mother? We will tell her the news together!"

Clara and Mary found Mrs. Price helping Aunt Catherine get settled upstairs. Mrs. Price was elated to hear the news. "I am glad for you, Miss Mary. Dr. Hamilton is a great man. I am sure that you will make each other very happy."

"Thank you, Mrs. Price. It means the world to me that you think so. You are the closest that I have to a mother left on this earth, and I am grateful to have your approval."

Downstairs in the servants' lobby, the housekeeper stood with a clipboard in her hand. She was conducting a meeting with the house staff which consisted of her younger sister Bridget, the cook Mrs. Malone, and the new housemaids, Jane and Nora. "Now that Miss Catherine has moved upstairs—"

A giggle erupted from the maids because Catherine used to work as the cook. Fiona continued solemnly. "As I said, Miss Catherine has moved upstairs and is to be addressed as such since she is a member of the family we serve. Miss Clara has announced that she would like to do more entertaining in the future. Nora, you will assist Mrs. Malone in the kitchen as needed until we hire a new kitchen maid. Bridget, you will attend to the girls as usual, but be aware that Miss Abigail does not intend to return for the next two days. You can assist Jane with housework in your extra time."

The staff nodded obediently and Fiona left the room to attend to other business. Nora, who shared a room with the housemaid Jane, began to pout after Fiona left. "Who does she think she is, telling me that I should help as a kitchen maid? I was the housekeeper at my last job. I should be attending the girls, if anyone. Or I should be the housekeeper here."

"How did you lose your job at the other house?" asked Jane, a slight girl with wide eyes. She looked up to Nora who had far more experience working in houses than Jane did.

"The family lost their money and could no longer pay the servants' wages," Nora answered sadly. "Still, after all my years of experience, it is insulting that I should be put to work in the kitchen. Bridget is only allowed to attend to the ladies because she is Fiona's sister. How is that fair? Fiona should not show favoritism just because they are related. Did you know that Bridget is only fourteen?"

"But she was working at the house before we were hired," Jane reminded her. "Perhaps that is why she gets to attend the girls."

"It's still no excuse," scowled Nora. She grudgingly went to work, making sure to give Jane an earful of her complaints whenever she had the opportunity.

Ethan and Abigail arrived at the manor house in Philadelphia late that night. Abigail covered her cheeks with her hands when she saw the house in the moonlight. "It is magnificent!" she cried. "I cannot believe it!"

Ethan smiled proudly. "I knew you would like the house. My aunt's housekeeper will let us in. Mrs. Davis is prepared for our visit."

"How wonderful," Abigail replied, taking Ethan's hand as he helped her down from the carriage. "I hope Mrs. Davis is amiable."

"She seemed alright when I met her," Ethan said. "My aunt seems to like her."

Ethan and Abigail found a plump elderly woman waiting for them by the front door. "Good evening, Mr. Smith, Mrs. Smith," the woman said. She led them up the staircase to a spacious room with high ceilings. "I hope this room will suit you," she said. "It is the finest room in the house."

"Thank you, Mrs. Davis," said Abigail. "It will do very nicely."

"Very good, Madam. I will be just downstairs if you need anything." Mrs. Davis left the room and closed the door behind her.

Abigail looked at Ethan and giggled. "She called me 'Madam'," she whispered amused.

Ethan looked around the room with his hands in his pockets. "This room is ridiculous," he finally said.

"What do you mean?"

"It feels like a giant cave, only worse. It's so—empty. Do you like it?" he asked her.

Abigail sighed. "I confess, I do not like it. Perhaps we could ask for something a bit more cozy."

"I don't want to bother Mrs. Davis again right now. She already looked tired from the day. We can sleep here tonight and ask for a different room tomorrow," Ethan suggested.

"Sounds perfect," Abigail agreed. But she lay awake throughout the night, feeling strange in the large, foreign room.

The next day, Mrs. Davis set out a splendid breakfast buffet in the dining room. Ethan and Abigail ate heartily while admiring their new surroundings. "They are treating us like royalty," Abigail remarked.

"The food is good," Ethan replied, filling his plate high at the buffet. After breakfast, they shyly asked Mrs. Davis to move them to a different room.

"The room I showed you to last night belonged to the former Master. Is it not to your liking, Madam?" she asked Abigail.

"It is a lovely room, Mrs. Davis, but we would like something cozier, if possible."

Mrs. Davis looked thoughtful. "Please follow me," she said, leading them to the opposite side of the manor house. "I will have the maids dust this room from top to bottom if it is to your liking."

Abigail looked helplessly at Ethan. The room was almost as large and empty as the one they had just declined, and Abigail was certain that Ethan would not feel comfortable in it. "Mrs. Davis, would you mind showing us to the smallest room in the house?" she asked.

Mrs. Davis's eyes grew wide. "The smallest, Madam?"

"If it is not too much trouble," Abigail added.

"Very well. Please come this way." They walked another distance to a delightful little room with sunlight streaming in through small windows.

"How darling!" exclaimed Abigail. "We would like to have this room. Did it belong to anyone in the family?"

"This room was used for a nursery, Madam," Mrs. Davis explained.

Abigail gave Ethan a look and giggled. "Thank you, Mrs. Davis," Ethan said quickly. "We won't make you parade us through the whole house. This room will do nicely."

When Mrs. Davis left the room, Abigail looked thoughtfully at Ethan. "Do you know what Clara told me before we left Davenport House? A telegram arrived announcing that Nellie Whitmore has been married. Did you know that Nellie once talked to her father about marrying you?"

Ethan shook his head and felt his face burning. "I never wanted to marry her."

"And now it is too late anyway, because you are all mine," Abigail said playfully, putting her arms around him.

Ethan hugged her tightly and turned serious. "I don't know what I would have done if you left on that ship with her. I don't know what I would do without you."

"I am still here. You need not worry about it anymore," Abigail assured him.

"But it wasn't the only time that I have nearly lost you. It's my greatest fear that something will happen to you, and I will lose you forever," he said, beginning to get choked up.

Abigail laid her head on his chest. "I am here right now. We have this lovely house to live in and neither of us is going anywhere. Right?"

Ethan nodded and held her tighter, unable to shake the ominous feeling that something was going to happen, and there was nothing he could do to prevent it.

The ladies at Davenport House were having lunch at the dining table. "Have you found anyone to be the new groundskeeper, Mother?" asked Clara.

"I interviewed a man just today, but I am not sure about him," Mrs. Price answered. "It will be difficult to find someone to fill John Smith's shoes."

"Yes it will," agreed Clara. "But I would not wish for Ethan to work double duty any longer than necessary. At least we may board Mary's horse when Ethan and Abigail move to the manor house. We will not need a stable boy any longer."

"Just what Ethan was worried about," Mary giggled. "Although he does not need to worry anymore, now that he has a grand house and stables of his own."

"We can offer the stable apartment as living quarters to the new groundskeeper," suggested Mrs. Price. "If we ever hire another manservant for the house, he may stay there as well. We will reserve downstairs for only the female staff."

"A good idea, Mother," Clara said.

Aunt Catherine ate quietly but plentifully at the breakfast table. "Are you plannin' another trip to New York?" she asked suddenly.

"I was hoping we could go again soon," Mrs. Price remarked. "Are you interested in going, Catherine?"

Catherine smiled. "It's been a dream of mine since I was a little girl."

"Then we must take you to New York just as soon as we can," Clara decided cheerfully. "Oh, but I cannot leave poor Mary here to plan the wedding by herself!"

Mary laughed. "Do not worry about me. Please, enjoy some time away. I can survive a few days on my own."

"Are you going into Yorktown to see William today?" asked Clara.

Mary sighed. "Not today, I'm afraid. He said he can come for dinner tomorrow night—if it is alright with you, Clara."

"William is welcome to the house at anytime, just as he was before," Clara answered. "Please do not hesitate to invite him whenever you wish."

"Thank you, Clara," Mary said gratefully.

Ethan and Abigail returned to Davenport House the next day. Abigail told Mary all about how they switched rooms at the manor house, and Mary told Abigail the news of her engagement. "I missed you dearly, Abigail," Mary admitted. "I don't know how I will live here without you."

"Won't you and William wish to live in the manor house when you are married?" she asked.

Mary shrugged. "I haven't spoken to him about it yet.

I don't know if he wants to move to Philadelphia, now that his clinic is established here."

"Oh, I see," Abigail replied. "Then I will come visit here as often as I am able. Ethan and I are staying in the stable apartment until a new groundskeeper is hired. So I am not leaving just yet."

Downstairs in the kitchen that night, Nora worked with Mrs. Malone to make dinner. Mrs. Malone noticed her scowling, and scolded Nora. "You won't have a job here long if you act like that."

"I didn't come here to be a lousy kitchen maid," Nora retorted. "I thought I would be attending the girls soon after I was hired. And now I'm serving the woman who used to be the cook! Everything about this house is backwards!"

Mrs. Malone turned away and said under her breath, "You have no idea."

CHAPTER 10

"You want me to make cakes for who?" questioned Mrs. Malone.

"Mr. Valenti. He is the neighbor as well as Miss Clara's chauffeur," Fiona explained.

"I know who the man is, but why should he have cakes from my kitchen?" the cook continued skeptically.

"Well—you see—" Fiona stammered. "It has become a bit of a tradition for the house to send sweets home with him. He has two small children, and he was very helpful with the horses and grounds while Mr. Ethan was away in Philadelphia."

Mrs. Malone raised her eyebrow at Fiona. "I suppose I could this one time. But if you want this to be a regular thing, I'll have to hear that the order came from Miss Clara."

Fiona nodded. "Thank you, Mrs. Malone." When she walked past the kitchen, she could hear Nora grumbling to Jane in the servants' lobby. "Haven't you any work to do, Nora?"

"I do," Nora grumbled. "But how long until a kitchen maid is hired?"

"The hiring of a groundskeeper is the house's priority now. Miss Clara, Mrs. Price, and Miss Catherine will soon leave for New York. You won't need to help in the kitchen then," Fiona assured her.

Bridget waited until she could talk to Fiona alone before she asked her question. "Fiona, have you heard anything from Miss Abigail? About me moving to the manor house with her?"

"She has not said anything to me," Fiona answered. "I thought she would speak to you about it first."

"I thought so too, but she has not mentioned anything since the wedding. I am worried that she has changed her mind," Bridget replied in concern.

"Miss Abigail has been busy," Fiona stated. "I'm certain she will ask you soon and then I'll have to find another housemaid. I will be sad to find your replacement."

"Who would attend to Miss Mary and Miss Clara after I leave?" asked Bridget.

"I can't decide. Nora has more experience, but I think Jane might be better suited."

"Nora will not like that at all," Bridget said, shaking her head. "She is already sore at me for attending to the girls. She calls me 'Child' when you are not around and often taunts me, insisting that I get special treatment for being your sister."

Fiona was surprised. "I had no idea she treated you poorly. I'm sorry, Bridget."

Bridget shrugged. "I didn't think it would matter if I was going away with Miss Abigail. I just hope that I hear from her about the manor house soon."

Fiona smiled at her sister. "I'm sure you will."

At the dinner table that evening, everyone wanted to

hear what Abigail thought of the manor house. "Did you stay in the house or the cottage?" asked Mary.

"We stayed in the house. It was even more beautiful than I imagined," she answered Mary, then turned to Clara. "I hope you may see it soon, Clara."

"I would like to after we return from New York," Clara replied. "It sounds fabulous!"

"We're goin' to New York tomorrow," Aunt Catherine beamed.

Mrs. Price then said, "I have news for everyone. I have interviewed a man called Mr. Harvey to take over as groundskeeper. He will arrive in the morning to begin, and Ethan may show him around the estate. Mr. Harvey has worked as a gardener in town."

Ethan looked up from his plate. "Is Mr. Harvey fit for an estate this size?"

"There is only one way to find out. There is a shortage of young men applying for positions because they are enlisting to help with the War effort. Mr. Harvey was available on short notice, and I did not wish to leave you without help while we are in New York," answered Mrs. Price.

"Thank you, Mrs. Price," Ethan said. He nudged Mary who was sitting beside him. "May I speak to you after dinner?" he whispered.

"Yes," Mary whispered back. She had not talked with Ethan much since he married Abigail, and Mary was glad that he wanted to talk to her again. They met in the library right after dinner. "This seems mysterious," Mary said with a twinkle in her eye. "What is it?"

Ethan laughed. "I only wanted to congratulate you on your engagement to William."

"Is that all? You could have said so at the dinner table, but thank you just the same," Mary replied.

"There is one more thing," he confessed. "Since Pa is gone, and he will not be here to give you away at your wedding—well—I wondered—"

"Do you wish to give me away?" Mary cried.

"Yes, if you want me to," he replied.

Mary put her arms around his neck and hugged him tightly. "I love you, dearest brother. Nothing would make me happier."

Clara was upstairs in her bedroom making last minute preparations for the trip when Abigail knocked on the open door. "Abigail, please come in," Clara said cheerfully.

"I have mended your gloves," Abigail told her, handing her the delicate lace gloves.

"Oh, thank you! These are my favorite and I was not sure if they could be saved."

"There is a request I would like to make, if it is alright," Abigail began.

"I am sure that my answer will be yes. You never ask for anything," giggled Clara.

Abigail smiled. "It is about the housemaid, Bridget. I would like to have her as my maid when we move to Philadelphia. Only if you are agreeable to it, of course."

"I will tell Fiona to make inquiries for a housemaid as soon as we get back. You must be quite taken with Bridget," Clara remarked.

"She is a dear girl. I do enjoy her company. Thank you, Clara, and I hope you have a brilliant time in New York."

The house was in a bustle the next day while Clara, Mrs. Price, and Aunt Catherine readied for their trip. Phillip Valenti, the chauffeur, loaded the ladies' suitcases onto the back of the car, and soon they were on their way to New York.

Mr. Harvey arrived early and Ethan showed him around the estate. Mr. Harvey appeared elderly, as if he experienced a hard life. Ethan became concerned that Mr. Harvey would not be able to keep up with work on the estate. He was slow and did not seem to catch on to what Ethan showed him over the next week. After Mr. Harvey went home for the night, Ethan retired to the stable apartment and walked right past Abigail and Bridget who were in the small sitting room. As Ethan collapsed on the bed, he could hear Abigail saying, "Now remember not to say a word to anyone downstairs. Clara should be the one to address the staff."

"I won't say anything," Bridget squealed in delight. "Thank you, Miss Abigail!" Bridget left the apartment and Abigail went into the bedroom to see Ethan.

"You look exhausted," she remarked. "Should I make you some tea?"

"I think I just need to sleep now. Maybe if I wake up extra early tomorrow, I can get some real work done before Mr. Harvey arrives. So what is the big secret with the housemaid?"

Abigail giggled. "Oh, that. She will be my maid at the manor house when we move into it. But I am beginning to worry that we might never leave if Mr. Harvey does not work out. What will you say about him to Mrs. Price when she returns?"

"I feel bad about it, but I have to tell her that Mr. Harvey just isn't fit to manage an estate this size. We've been needing to rebuild part of the fence around the pasture, but he takes so long to do anything, we've not even begun to work on it. I'm sorry, Abigail. We won't be able to leave just yet."

"I understand," Abigail sighed. "Poor Mr. Harvey. I hope he finds another job in town." She looked at Ethan for a response, but he was already asleep on the bed. Abigail smiled and kissed his forehead before heading to the desk in the sitting room. She took out a pen and paper and began to write.

Much to everyone's surprise, Clara and Mrs. Price returned to Davenport House—without Aunt Catherine. Clara announced with glee what had happened in New York. "Can you believe it? My Aunt Catherine has married!" she exclaimed during lunch.

"To who?" Mary laughed.

"It was a man she met the day we arrived at the hotel. They fell in love and and decided they will live on his river boat on the Mississippi!"

Mary laughed. "Who could have guessed that Catherine would be the next person in the house to get married? What a surprise!"

"I am only happy to see my sister happy," smiled Mrs. Price. "It amazes me how this house and the people in it are always changing. Abigail, will you be off to the manor house, now that Clara and I have returned?"

"Um—not just yet," Abigail stammered.

Ethan looked uncomfortably at Mrs. Price. "Mr. Harvey is not quite working out…"

"I am sorry to hear that," Mrs. Price replied. "Could it be that he needs more time to adjust?"

"I have shown him the best I can. It might not hurt to put out inquiries for the position again," Ethan told her solemnly.

"I see. I will do so as soon as we get settled in. We will

at least give Mr. Harvey the chance to keep working until the position is filled," Mrs. Price said thoughtfully.

Ethan nodded, but Abigail heard him groaning under his breath. She quickly turned to Mrs. Price. "I am certain that Mr. Harvey will appreciate you thinking of him. We will stay at Davenport House until the position is filled."

"How are your wedding plans coming along, Miss Mary?" asked Mrs. Price.

"I'm afraid I have not made any progress while Clara was away," Mary answered.

"Then we will start again first thing in the morning," Clara stated. "Not to worry, Mary. Your wedding will be spectacular!"

"Not so fast," Mrs. Price said sternly. "Your studies must come first, then the wedding planning."

Clara giggled. "Mother has made me promise to take courses by correspondence to learn more about business. I did not think that I would like it much at first, but now am beginning to enjoy it. Not to worry, Mother. I can do both at once."

Mrs. Price smiled at her daughter. "I have every faith that you will."

Clara spent the next days delving into her studies and helping Mary plan the wedding. Mary decided to have the ceremony in the little church in Yorktown, then the wedding reception at the house. Clara was only too happy to arrange for the flowers and cake.

Mary was meeting with the minister in the drawing room to discuss the dates available for the ceremony. She became concerned when Abigail unexpectedly burst into the room. "What is it?" Mary asked, seeing that she was in distress.

Abigail looked back and forth between the minister and Mary. "Where is Clara?" she asked suddenly.

"I think she is upstairs in her room. What has happened?"

Abigail did not answer. She left Mary abruptly and hurried upstairs to find Clara. After Mary had finished speaking with the minister, she went upstairs to find Abigail. Clara was alone in her room, sorting through her wardrobe. "Mary," she smiled upon seeing her enter. "What do you think about this cheerful yellow gown for me to wear for the wedding? Oh, how did everything go with the minister?"

"The dress is lovely, and the meeting was fine. But I wondered if Abigail was alright. Did she come up to see you?"

Clara frowned when she answered. "She did. She asked if I would let her move back into the house."

"Oh, is that all," Mary said in relief. "She has likely become tired of living in the stable."

"But Mary, she seemed rather upset. I had the feeling that she wanted to move back into the house—without Ethan," Clara said quietly.

Mary's mouth was open in shock. "There must be a reasonable explanation," she decided.

Clara looked helplessly at Mary. "Abigail refused to speak about it. She asked if she could have dinner sent to her old room tonight."

"I wonder what could have happened today," Mary thought aloud.

"Phillip drove her to town earlier," Clara said. "Perhaps something upsetting happened while she was out."

"I see," Mary nodded. "I will go to her." She went to Abigail's room and knocked on the door. "It's me, Abigail. May I come in?"

"I'm very tired, Mary. Please let me rest," Abigail called back. Mary slowly walked away from the door and down the long hallway, hoping that her friend would be all right.

On the estate grounds, Mrs. Price ventured out to find Ethan. She could see him working intently and it startled him to see Mrs. Price standing there. "What is it?" he asked gruffly.

Mrs. Price was taken aback by his greeting, but remained calm. "Mr. Harvey has said that you told him to leave the estate. Is that true?"

"He's just making more work for me," Ethan grunted, not looking Mrs. Price in the eyes. "He's too old."

"Just how old do you think Mr. Harvey is?" Mrs. Price asked.

"I don't know—seventy?" guessed Ethan.

Mrs. Price raised her eyebrow skeptically. "He is fifty, same age as your pa."

"Oh. Well Pa was different, he knew this estate like the back of his hand," Ethan scowled.

"Your pa took great care of the estate and I know it must be difficult to think of him as being replaceable. In the meantime, I have given Mr. Harvey severance wages because we did not keep him as long as we intended. Are you certain you wish to do the work by yourself until a new man is hired?"

"I'm certain," Ethan responded in a low voice. "I have to get back to work."

Mrs. Price nodded. "As you wish."

Later that evening, neither Ethan nor Abigail were at the dinner table. Their glaring absence was felt by all in the dining room. "I wonder why Ethan has not come for dinner tonight," Clara remarked.

"Ethan was in a sore mood today," said Mrs. Price. "He nearly bit my head off when I talked to him about Mr. Harvey. Ethan sent him home without speaking to me about it first."

Mary was perplexed. "That does not sound like Ethan at all. I wonder what is bothering him."

"I'm sure it is because he thinks no one is good enough to replace his pa," Mrs Price replied.

"Mother," Clara sent gently. "You should probably know that Abigail has moved back into the house. She is having dinner in her room tonight."

"Oh?" Mrs. Price said, her eyes growing wide. "Only Abigail?"

"It would seem that way," Clara replied, looking down at her plate. Even though they all wondered, no one said another word about Ethan and Abigail for the rest of the evening.

Chapter 11

Abigail's meals were sent to her room over the next several days, and when Mary tried to visit her again, she was not there. "Is Abigail in the house?" Mary asked Clara in the drawing room.

"Phillip has taken her to town again," answered Clara. "She seemed to be doing better today when I saw her."

"I was going to ask if she could help me fit my dress, but I am worried that I would be bothering her," Mary explained. She heard Abigail come through the door just then. Mary went into the Hall to meet her. "Good afternoon," she said. "Did you get everything you needed in town?"

"Yes, I did, thank you," answered Abigail, but her hands were empty. "How are your wedding plans coming, Mary?"

"They are going well. I hoped I could ask you about fitting the dress for me in a few places…" Mary said hesitantly.

"I would be glad to. Just bring the dress to my room and we will be sure that it fits perfectly," Abigail answered her with a smile.

Mary smiled too, thinking for a moment that

everything might be alright after all. "I will bring it to your room tonight."

Later that week, Mary was preparing to leave for Yorktown to see the minister. She stopped by Abigail's room before she left. "Good morning. I am going into town and wanted to ask if you needed anything."

"It is good of you to ask, Mary. Are you going to see William?" asked Abigail.

"Not today. I need to meet with the minister at the church, but I can stop by a shop on the way back if there's anything you need," offered Mary.

"Actually, I would like to go into Yorktown with you, if it is alright. I can get what I need while you meet with the minister," Abigail said. "If you don't mind waiting a moment for me to get ready."

Mary was delighted. "I am glad you want to come. It has been ages since we have gone anywhere together. I will be waiting in the car with Phillip."

"Thank you, Mary. I'll be right out," Abigail replied. The girls were soon on their way to Yorktown in the car. After Phillip dropped Mary off at the church, he turned to Abigail in the backseat.

"Does Mary know?" he asked.

Abigail shook her head. "I'd like to keep it that way for now."

Phillip nodded. "I won't say anything."

"Thank you," Abigail sighed in relief. "But will you drive me closer to the general store? I need to make it look as though I came into town to buy something."

"Of course," replied Phillip. "Anything you need."

When Mary was finished meeting the minister, she went

out to where Abigail and Phillip were waiting in the car. "Did you have enough time to visit the shops?" she asked Abigail.

"Yes, thank you. How was the meeting with the minister?"

"It was wonderful. We have set a date, and can now really begin to plan," answered Mary in excitement. "Clara will be thrilled."

"I am so glad for you, Mary," Abigail smiled.

Just after Mary climbed into the car, she noticed a young woman across the street who appeared to be staring directly at her. Mary had never seen the woman before, yet she was now waving in Mary's direction. Mary waved back confused, wondering if she knew the woman from somewhere but had forgotten. Then the woman called out, "Abigail!" Mary turned to Abigail who was watching in horror as the woman approached from across the street.

"Phillip, drive us home—now!" urged Abigail. Phillip was startled and pushed the gas pedal, leaving the woman standing bewildered in the street.

"Who was that?" asked Mary.

Abigail sank into her seat. "I don't wish to speak about her, Mary." Abigail turned her face away, leaving Mary to wonder why it made her upset to see the woman. When they arrived back at Davenport House, Abigail went straight into the house to her bedroom. Mary decided to go to the stable in the hopes of seeing Ethan. He was rotating the hay bales from a fresh delivery. He barely noticed when Mary walked in.

"Ethan?" she called timidly.

"Good afternoon, Mary," he said distractedly without pausing from his work.

"You are working too hard. I wonder if we should board the horses for now so your load will be lightened."

"I like it this way," mumbled Ethan. "That Mr. Harvey fellow slowed me down, but I'm almost caught up."

"I think you should go see Abigail," Mary said.

Ethan stopped what he was doing and turned to face Mary. "Did she ask for me?"

"No, but she seems to be troubled. She saw a woman in town today who tried to talk to her, but Abigail became upset and refused to see her."

"Hm," was all Ethan responded, resuming his work with the hay.

"Do you know what it could be about?" persisted Mary.

"You'd have to talk to her about it," Ethan replied.

Mary felt awkward as the distance between them felt greater than ever. She glanced at the floor of the stable where the new fence boards were stacked, and she decided to change the subject. "I see the boards have been delivered for the new fence," she remarked.

"I'm working on it," Ethan muttered.

"Perhaps Phillip could help—"

"I said I'm working on it, Mary!" Ethan snapped. Mary felt tears filling her eyes and turned to leave. "Wait," Ethan called after her. "I'm sorry. I shouldn't have said it like that."

"I don't understand what is happening," Mary whimpered, feeling the tears spill over. "We used to be able to tell each other anything. Just days ago you said you would give me away at my wedding, but now it is like we are strangers. If you only tell me what is troubling you, maybe I can help." Ethan walked over to her and put his arms around her. Mary could feel his body begin to shake with cries and his tears fell on her shoulder. "I am sorry for whatever has happened—whatever is making you feel this way. Please tell me what I may do to help."

Ethan finally pulled away and wiped his face. "There's nothing you can do. Not for this. Just make sure that Abigail is alright and don't worry about me." Ethan returned to his work, and Mary could sense that their conversation was over. She quietly left the stable.

Later in the afternoon, Mrs. Price approached Ethan in the stable. "Ethan," she called, walking in with a young man. "This is Samuel. He has applied for the position and I told him we will try him out for a few weeks. He is only seventeen," she added with a smile. She could tell that Ethan was in a better mood than the last time they spoke.

Ethan reached out to shake his hand. "Nice to meet you, Samuel," he greeted.

"I am glad to meet you," Samuel answered.

"Do I know you from somewhere? You look familiar, but I don't remember where I've seen you," Ethan said.

Samuel laughed. "No, Sir. This is the first time we've met."

"I will leave you two to get acquainted," Mrs. Price said before walking away.

"Should I call you Mr. Ethan, or Mr. Smith, or—sorry I don't really know how these things work," Samuel admitted.

"Just call me Ethan. Do you know how to saddle a horse?" he asked.

"Sure do," Samuel replied eagerly, lifting a saddle off the ground as if it weighed nothing. He expertly saddled one of the horses while Ethan saddled the other.

"Well, let's get going. There are five hundred acres and we need to be quick if we're to get a good look around before dark," Ethan said.

Samuel was already on his horse before Ethan finished his sentence. "Just lead the way," he replied. "I'm ready."

In the servants' quarters of Davenport House, Fiona

was sitting at the desk in her office when Nora approached her. "What is it, Nora?" Fiona asked impatiently.

"I wished to talk to you about Bridget," she said. "I know she's your sister, but perhaps she's not the maid best suited to attend to the ladies."

"And I suppose you want to recommend yourself for the position?" Fiona responded.

"I have many years experience, you see. I've been trained in styling ladies' hair even. Miss Abigail has chosen to style her own hair, but I think that she, Miss Mary, and Miss Clara could benefit from a maid who knows what she's doing," Nora replied. "Perhaps this is not the best circumstance for you to show favoritism."

Fiona sighed in irritation. "Bridget has been attending the girls for months now. You cannot tell me how to do my job, Nora." Nora stared at Fiona, making her squirm uncomfortably in her seat. Fiona finally looked up and asked, "Have you more to say?"

"Now that you mention it, I'm not sure that you are the best suited to be housekeeper here."

"I beg your pardon!" Fiona exclaimed.

"Your sister is not the only one you show favoritism to. You have forced Mrs. Malone to make special food for the chauffeur as well," Nora stated. "Isn't he the same man that Miss Clara has thrown over? Do you think she would be happy to hear that he has been receiving extra things from the kitchen? In the house I used to manage, what you have done would be called stealing. I would have sacked any of my maids caught doing such a thing."

Fiona was aghast at the suggestion. "Well I—" she stammered. "It was at Miss Mary's request to send food to the neighbors—when she was still Mistress of the house."

"But now you are employed by Miss Clara. She has been taking courses in business to take every possible measure to save money. I understand that the chauffeur is attractive to look at, but I wonder how proper it is for you to continue showing him special treatment."

Fiona hated that she could feel her face burning red just then. "What is the point of saying these things to me, Nora?"

Nora shrugged. "I am giving you the chance to make your bad habits right. It is clear that I should be attending the ladies upstairs. You might want to rethink whether you want to be known as a housekeeper who plays favorites with the staff—especially the male staff," she added.

"I do not appreciate what you are implying," Fiona stated, trying to remain calm. "You do your job and let me do mine. Otherwise I will have to discipline you for impertinence."

"Well then, since you are suddenly concerned with ethics, I'll be happy to tell the Mistress that her own housekeeper has been stealing from her. She might be interested to hear how she can save money if she only had an honest woman doing the job." Nora turned on her heel and left the room. Fiona sat flustered at her desk, afraid of what Nora might do next.

Fiona rushed upstairs to the library, where Clara was updating the ledgers, and approached her apprehensively. "Miss Clara, may I speak to you for a moment?"

"Yes, what is it?"

"You see, one of the maids used to be a housekeeper in a grand house like this. She has training in attending ladies with their hair and clothes. I wanted to ask if you would prefer to have her attending you over Bridget."

"Oh," Clara said in surprise. "I would like to try new things with my hair. But which maid is this?"

"It is Nora, Miss Clara."

Clara wrinkled her nose. "I don't know about her. I have an odd feeling when she is about. I am sad to be losing Bridget because I already know her and trust her. You remember that I had a terrible experience with a maid who could not be trusted."

"I remember, Miss Clara. I will recommend Jane to attend you when Bridget leaves, if you wish. Unless I find someone more suitable."

"Yes, I think that should work out nicely. Thank you, Fiona," Clara said. She then began to rifle through papers on the desk.

Fiona cleared her throat. "There is one more thing, Miss Clara," she said nervously. "On two occasions since you have been Mistress, I have asked the cook to make special desserts for Mr. Valenti. The first time was when he helped us maids in the servants' quarters when Stuart was bothering us. The second time was when he looked after the grounds while Mr. Ethan was away. Miss Mary allowed for food to be sent with Mr. Valenti in the past, but I realized that I never received your permission to do so."

Clara looked at her compassionately. "My mother told me about Stuart bothering you, and for that I am sorry. I know this house has been turned upside down many times over and it must be as confusing to the staff as it is for the rest of us. Thank you for telling me about the desserts you have sent to the Valentis, and you need not worry about it. Please ask me if you wish to do so in the future so that I may better track the house expenses."

"Yes, of course. Thank you, Miss Clara." Fiona breathed a sigh of relief and returned to the servants' quarters.

After showing Samuel around the estate, Ethan slept

hard in his room above the stable that night. He woke up to sunlight streaming in through the window and realized that it was much later in the morning than he usually began work. He got dressed and went to the second bedroom that Samuel was occupying. "Sorry I overslept, we gotta get to work now," Ethan said through the door after knocking. There was no answer, so Ethan opened the door. He only saw a neatly made bed in the room, but no sign of Samuel. Ethan went down the stairs to look for him. Samuel was busy taking the horses out to the pasture. "Hold on, we shouldn't do that yet," Ethan told him. "First we need to—" Ethan stopped talking when he did not see the fence boards on the stable floor. "What happened to the boards that were here?"

"I saw a weak spot in the fence that needed fixin' and I worried that the horses would get out," answered Samuel. "I guessed that was what the boards were for, so I got the fence rails up this morning."

"You did?" Ethan asked, his eyebrows raised in surprise. The fence was a big job that should have taken all day, so Ethan was worried that it would be poorly done. He went out to the pasture to inspect the fence and Samuel followed close behind him. Ethan grabbed the posts and rails to determine how sturdy they were, then stood back to admire the fence. "You did a fine job, Samuel."

"Thank you," he beamed. "Should I bring the other horses out now?"

Ethan laughed. "Yes, you should. But you won't have to manage the horses after I leave. I am taking two of them with me, and the other one will be boarded at a ranch in Yorktown. You'll only have the grounds to do."

"I am sure I can manage both the grounds and one horse if Mary wants to keep Dolly here," Samuel assured him.

Ethan gave Samuel a confused look. "How did you know about Mary and her horse?"

"Didn't you say something about it last night?"

Ethan sighed and shook his head. "I can't remember what I said. This week has been…" he trailed off.

"I'll get the other horses and then you can tell me what to do next." Samuel went back to the stable. Ethan sighed in relief that Davenport House may have just found its new groundskeeper.

Later that evening, Ethan dressed in a suit and tie for dinner. He went into the house early and found Mrs. Price in the library. "Ethan," she greeted in surprise. "You are looking well tonight."

"I'm sorry for the way I acted the other day," Ethan told her, looking ashamed. "I should've talked to you before sending Mr. Harvey home, and I should've been civil when you came to ask me about it."

"Well it's in the past now," Mrs. Price replied peaceably. "I am glad to see you have come to have dinner with us tonight. You've not taken a rest in a long while."

"I guess my hunger got the better of me," Ethan replied shyly. "I also needed to speak to you. Firstly to apologize, and second to tell you…Samuel might be the right one for the job. I'm ashamed to admit he may even be more qualified than me."

"Well! It is the highest recommendation I have ever heard," Mrs. Price stated. "I told the boy that his employment here would be on trial for weeks. When you are certain, Ethan, you may tell him that his employment will be permanent. You must be pleased that it means you can move to your house in Philadelphia now."

Ethan looked at the floor. "I don't know when we will

move, Mrs. Price. We might stay here for awhile, if it's alright with you and Clara."

Mrs. Price looked at him compassionately. "You may stay as long as you need."

Abigail was not at dinner that night, but everyone else seemed to be in high spirits. William told them about the his new intern from Pittsburgh, and Mrs. Price announced that the new groundskeeper was going to be hired permanently.

"We will miss you and Abigail, now that you are moving," Clara said to Ethan. But he was looking down at his plate.

"Ethan has offered to stay as long as necessary to ensure Samuel is trained for the job," Mrs. Price stated. Ethan gave her a look of gratitude.

"I have news," Mary said, grinning at William who sat across from her. "I met with the minister, and we have set a date for our wedding!"

Cheers erupted from around the table and William smiled endearingly at Mary, wishing he could be close enough to hold her hand. Everyone ate their food heartily, and soon Mary was with William at the front door, telling him goodnight.

"Will you come again for dinner tomorrow?" she asked him.

"I am planning on it," he replied. "May I kiss you goodbye?"

"I won't let you leave until you do," Mary answered.

William chuckled as he leaned in to kiss her, and said exactly what was on his mind. "I cannot wait to marry you."

Chapter 12

Mary and Clara were alone at the breakfast table the next morning. "I wonder why Mother is not here for breakfast," Clara said curiously. "It has been lonely enough without Abigail to eat with us."

"A strange thing happened in town with Abigail," Mary said. "I wish I could help in some way, only I do not know what is wrong with her."

"Neither do I," Clara said. "She received several letters from her family in Johnstown last week. Perhaps something has happened to one of them."

"It would be terrible if it had," Mary thought aloud. "But surely if it was a problem with her family, she would have told us. And it does not explain why she has moved into the house without Ethan."

"I do not mean to be a gossip, but I wonder if Phillip knows something," Clara remarked. "He has been lately taking her to town. I did not think it right to ask him, though."

"It probably is not," Mary agreed. "I think I will ask Abigail if she would like to ride the horses with me after breakfast. We will not have many more opportunities before she moves away."

"Have a good time, Mary," said Clara. "I'm going to check on Mother, then I will be busy with my studies for the rest of the day."

Mary went to Abigail's room and knocked on the door. "Come in," said Abigail, sitting up on the bed. "Oh, good morning, Mary. I thought you were Bridget."

"I hope it is still alright that I came in."

Abigail giggled. "Of course it is. I am glad to see you."

Mary smiled hopefully. "I came to invite you for a ride with me. It might be just the thing to cheer you up, and we do not need to talk about anything."

"You are kind to ask, but I'm afraid I cannot ride today," Abigail answered sadly. She was unable to say more because Clara suddenly burst into the room in distress.

"I cannot wake her, Mary!" she cried.

Mary's heart was racing as she hurried to Mrs. Price's bedroom with Clara. Mrs. Price lay on the bed, her lifeless body cold to the touch. Clara and Mary exchanged horrified looks. "Is she dead?" Clara whimpered.

Mary could not bring herself to respond. She began to tremble, but was able to whisper the words, "We must telephone William."

"I have just called him," Abigail said from the doorway. "He is on his way now." The three girls surrounded the bed and stared in silence where Mrs. Price lay. They watched in hopefulness for any sign of breath or movement from her—any hint at all that she was only in a deep sleep, and not truly gone forever. But as the girls waited in anguish for William to arrive, they only witnessed the complete stillness of Mrs. Price's body.

William nodded sadly to confirm that Mrs. Price had indeed passed away during the night. "I am sorry, Clara," he said gently. "It was her heart. There was nothing that could be done to save her."

"But she was fine just yesterday! You were here last night—you saw how well she looked!"

"It is a shock to lose someone so suddenly, and I am sorry for your loss," William replied in sorrow. "I hope you may find peace in knowing that your mother did not suffer, but passed in her sleep."

"I can't believe it," Clara said, lowering herself onto the bed. "I just can't believe it." Abigail draped a shawl around Clara's shoulders and offered to inform the staff. When Abigail returned with a tray of tea, Mary and William left for the sitting room.

"I am sorry, Mary. I know you admired her a great deal," William said painfully. He put his arms around her as they stood there.

"She was the closest that I had to a mother," Mary answered. "I cannot remember a day of my life without Mrs. Price. When Clara is ready, I will suggest that the burial be beside Mr. Davenport in the family cemetery."

"It is as it should be," William said, still holding her. "Mrs. Price said she wished to be buried next to Clara's father."

Mary pulled away and looked at him curiously. "How would you know that?"

William swallowed the lump in his throat. "She told me, Mary. She said that she could not be by his side in life, but that she wished to in death."

Mary looked at him incredulously. "Why would she say such a thing to you?"

"She has been my patient for some time. She knew that her heart was weak, and told me of what she wished for her burial for when the time came," William explained.

Mary backed away from him. "You knew about this?" she demanded.

"Yes," he replied.

Mary gasped. "For how long?"

William cringed as he thought about it. "It has been months."

Mary was aghast. "You can't be serious! You have known that she was dying for months and never thought to mention it once?"

William looked helplessly at Mary. "I couldn't tell you, as much as I wanted to. Mrs. Price wanted it to be this way. She did not want to be fussed over. It was her decision whether to make her condition known to her family."

Mary shook with anger. "How could you! Do you know how we found out that she was ill? Clara found her own mother dead this morning. Now she will have to live with that horrid memory for the rest of her life! What did you think it would do to us to find out like this? If you warned us, we could have been prepared!"

"It would be against the law and against my conscience," William told her. "It is what I meant when I said there were things about my job that I could not tell you about."

The more he spoke, the more furious Mary became. "I cannot believe that you had dinner with us just last night, pretending as if nothing were wrong! How could you keep such a thing from me? I know the law does not permit you to discuss your patients, but surely this was the exception! You have robbed her own daughter of the chance to say goodbye!"

"I know you're upset right now. You have every reason to be, and it will be an emotional time for everyone in the house. Perhaps I should leave now and we will talk later," William said.

"Wait—there is one thing I want to know before you leave," Mary said, feeling her fists clench at her sides. "If I was already your wife, *then* would you have told me about this?"

William swallowed the lump in his throat. He had never seen Mary this angry before and he was worried about how she would react to his answer. "No, I would not."

Mary crossed her arms over her chest and felt tears of rage blinding her. "I suppose I did not know what I was agreeing to when I said I could be a doctor's wife. I don't see how I could live with you, now that I know you could keep such secrets from me." Mary turned her back to William and faced the window.

"I need you to understand this, Mary," he said. "Now is not the time to make decisions about us."

"I have already made my decision," Mary replied, still facing the window. "I want you to leave and never come back." She heard the double doors open and close behind her, then she turned around to find herself alone in the room.

Abigail heard the shouting from the sitting room, then observed that William was hurrying out of the house. "William!" she called before he reached the front door.

He turned around with tears in his eyes. "Are you alright, Abigail?" he asked.

"Don't worry about me just now," she said. "What did Mary say to you?"

Tears rolled down his face as he replied. "She told me to leave and never come back. She does not understand."

Abigail gasped. "Oh no! She surely does not know what she is saying. She is only in shock over Mrs. Price!"

"I can't say I blame her for hating me," William said mournfully. "I have been in agony every time I have been with Mary, not being able to tell her."

"I will talk to her," Abigail said. "She needs time to understand what has happened, and it has surely brought back memories of when she found poor Mr. Davenport."

"She is angry with me, Abigail, and I have to leave now. Please, take care of yourself." William turned to go out the door.

Downstairs in the servants' lobby, the housemaids stood in silence as Fiona told them the news of Mrs. Price passing. No one could believe it, and Mrs. Malone began to cry.

"We must be sensitive to the family during this difficult time," Fiona instructed. "We will deliver meals to their rooms until further notice. We will take them fresh trays of tea throughout the day. Let us not wait for them to ask for it, but rather let us anticipate that they will require it at regular intervals." The servants agreed and Fiona took Nora aside. "Nora, I must ask that you help in the kitchen again. Mrs. Malone worked with Mrs. Price for many years and she now needs our support." Nora did not answer, but Fiona could tell that she was not pleased with the request. Ethan and Samuel came through the servants' entrance just then and met Fiona in the lobby.

"We heard about Mrs. Price," Ethan said, hanging his head. "I am sorry for the loss of a great woman." Fiona nodded solemnly, and also looked curiously at the young man who walked in with Ethan.

"I have come to introduce Samuel to you. Mrs. Price hired him to manage the estate grounds." He turned to Samuel. "Fiona is the housekeeper. You will come to her if you have questions about the estate after I am gone."

"I am pleased to meet you, Samuel," Fiona greeted.

"Likewise," Samuel replied. Fiona thought at once that Samuel looked familiar, but she did not know where she could have known him from. After he and Ethan left the servants' quarters, Fiona went to ask her sister. "Bridget, do we know that young man?"

"I think so," Bridget answered slowly. "Perhaps we have seen him around town."

"Perhaps," Fiona said thoughtfully, but she was sure there was another reason she felt like she already knew him.

Mary went to Mrs. Price's room and sat down quietly beside Clara. "Is there anything I may do for you?"

Clara shook her head. "At least she did not suffer," she said. "I cannot notify Aunt Catherine until she sends us an address. I suppose we should call the undertaker and arrange the burial."

"We will do those things when you are ready," Mary said gently. "There is something I should tell you that William has told me. He said your mother wished to be buried beside your father."

"William said that? How would he know?" asked Clara.

Mary sighed heavily, and continued in the softest tone she could manage. "Apparently, your mother was seeing him for her heart condition. She knew that she was dying and told him her last wishes. She said that she did not want us to make a fuss over her being ill."

Clara managed a slight smile. "That does sound just like Mother. I can picture her saying it right now."

"I scolded William for keeping such a secret from us," resumed Mary. "I told him not to come back to the house."

"Mary, you didn't!" Clara responded. "How could you say such a thing to the man who has done so much for us?"

"Do you mean that you are not angry with him for withholding what he knew?" Mary asked perplexed.

"How could I be? It is against the law, not to mention that it was my mother's wish that we not know in advance," Clara answered.

Mary sat quietly for Clara's sake, but did not feel any change in her anger or decision to break with William.

Later that evening, Ethan carried two shovels with him when he approached Samuel in the stable. "I'm sorry I have to ask you to work late when you have only just started. If you come with me, I'll show you the place where Clara has asked us to prepare the grave."

Samuel nodded solemnly and followed Ethan past the woods into a small clearing. There was a wrought iron fence and gate forming the perimeter around several headstones. Ethan showed him where they would begin digging beside the headstone that read *JAMES DAVENPORT*. Samuel looked at Ethan and could tell at once how weary he was. "I can take care of this myself," Samuel told him. "I've dug a grave before."

"It will take you all night if you work by yourself," Ethan argued.

But Samuel insisted. "It is the least I can do for the lady who gave me the chance to work here. Why don't you go be with your wife, and I will see that the grave is finished by morning."

Ethan was about to argue again, but his muscles ached and his eyelids weighed heavy. He was not sure if he had it in him to be stubborn just then. "Thank you, Samuel," he acquiesced. "I don't know how we got so lucky to have you come work here, but I'm sure glad we did."

The day of the burial was dark and dreary. A light sprinkle

of rain fell over the freshly dug earth in the Davenport cemetery. The undertaker brought a casket to the house, and William arrived shortly after him. Mary came down the staircase in her black mourning dress and was shocked to see William standing there. "Clara asked me to come," he explained quietly. Mary nodded but did not speak to him. She instead went into the drawing room where Clara and Abigail were waiting sorrowfully.

The minister and the undertaker together with William and Ethan carried the casket back down the staircase. The girls followed them to the cemetery and the minister said a few words as they lowered the casket into the ground. Ethan stood with his arm around Abigail. Mary wished for a moment that she was not standing there alone in the rain. She glanced at William, who looked sadly at the casket in the ground.

After the burial, everyone walked back to the house. Mary went straight to her room while the rest of them had a quiet meal in the dining room. Mary changed into her night-clothes and lay in bed, hoping that if she only slept tonight, tomorrow would not seem so grim.

She woke early the next morning and left her room to ask one of the maids for breakfast. Mary reached the upstairs landing just in time to see Ethan leaving the house. Bridget had just come up the servants' stairs and was walking toward Mary. "Bridget, was that Ethan who just left?"

"It was, Miss Mary," Bridget responded. "Mr. Ethan comes to visit Miss Abigail every morning at this time."

"He does?" asked Mary. "I did not realize. Is Abigail awake now?"

"She is, Miss. I am just bringing her a tray of breakfast," Bridget answered.

"Would you bring up another tray for me? I will take this one to her," said Mary.

"Very good, Miss." Bridget soon disappeared down the servants' stairs.

"Abigail, I have your breakfast tray," Mary announced, entering Abigail's room.

"Thank you, Mary. I have been wanting to speak to you anyway," Abigail said.

Mary sat in the chair next to Abigail's bed. "What is it?"

"It's about William…"

Mary felt her heart drop to her stomach and she took a deep breath. "Never have I felt so betrayed by someone I loved so much," she said, her voice cracking with emotion.

"I understand why you are upset…but are you certain that you no longer want to marry him?" Abigail questioned gently.

"It worries me that he can keep such secrets from me and not even be sorry about it. If he does not tell the truth about this, what else might he keep from me?"

Abigail sighed. "I believe that William is a trustworthy man, and would only keep something from you if it was honorable to do so. It is part of his profession. It is part of what makes him a good doctor."

"I know you are trying to make peace between me and William, but I don't think there is anything you can say that will make me think what he did was the right thing. Even Clara does not seem to mind that he didn't warn us. I get the feeling that both of you think I am wrong in this," Mary said honestly.

"You are wrong, Mary."

"I am?" Mary asked, suddenly feeling panicked. It was not often that she was called out by one of her friends.

Abigail nodded, casting her glance toward the blanket in front of her. "I am going to tell you something now. I had not planned on saying anything to you yet, but I think the time is right." Abigail took a deep breath before she continued. "You see, not long ago, I realized that I was pregnant."

Mary looked surprised. "Oh Abigail, how wonderful."

Abigail looked pained as she continued. "Please, let me finish what I have to say. Otherwise I will burst into tears now and not be able to get through it."

Mary's countenance fell and she became serious, worrying about what Abigail might say next.

"The baby didn't survive," Abigail stammered while a tear rolled down her cheek. "I went to see William as soon as it happened. He helped me to understand that it happens to many women, and he has given me medicine for the pain. It is why I moved back into the house. William said that I should not take the stairs so often, but instead let the servants bring me what I need. I have been seeing him all this while at the clinic. But I know he has not said a word to you about it."

Mary was stunned and mournful at the same time. "No, William has not said anything," she whispered.

"And he has done the right thing by not telling you— even though he loves you more than anything in the world, and he knows that you and I are so close. There are things that are not his right to tell. I also love you dearly, but I was not ready for you to know this. You were so happy about your engagement and making plans for your wedding…I could not bear to think that you might become as sad as I have been. I planned to tell you after—after your wedding."

"Is there anything I can do to help? Will you be alright?" Mary asked in concern.

Abigail shook her head. "I am not alright, but I want you

to be. I wish that everyone in the house would go on like usual and not worry about Ethan and me. It is better to keep this just between us and grieve quietly. I don't know how else to explain it."

"You do not have to explain," Mary said compassionately. She sat quietly for awhile, feeling helpless, sad, and guilty. "I think I understand why you told me this now. It is a sad time for the house on all fronts, but I will do as you wish by going on as usual."

"Thank you. That would be easiest for me," Abigail said, looking down in sorrow. "I am going to see William tomorrow to ask if I have healed enough to take the carriage to Philadelphia. I do wish to move to the manor house as soon as possible. I suppose we must wait until the new groundskeeper position is settled so that Ethan is free to leave." Clara entered the room just then. She seemed surprisingly cheerful.

"Oh Mary, you are here too. Look what I have found in Mother's things," she said, holding out three envelopes. "She has written these letters for us. I have already read mine, and Mother said the dearest things to me! I am sure to treasure it always. These two are addressed to you and Abigail." Clara gave them the envelopes and stood there as they were read.

"How good of her," Abigail smiled as she read the kind words from Mrs. Price. "What does yours say, Mary?"

Mary had tears falling down her face as she read the message over and over. "I will let you read it tomorrow," she promised. "There is something I must do first."

Chapter 13

"Well Samuel, I think it's safe to say that you don't need to finish the trial period that Mrs. Price set for you. I believe you are the right man for the job, and I never thought I'd say those words after working here with my pa all my life. I am going to tell Clara that you are ready to be the groundskeeper."

Samuel was beaming. "Thank you, Ethan," he said, giving him a hearty handshake.

"Just one final thing before I tell her—are you sure you won't be enlisting to fight in this War, leaving the ladies in search of another groundskeeper?" Ethan asked seriously.

Samuel laughed. "No Sir, not me. My pa says that the English deserve what they get from the Germans, and I agree with him."

"That is just what my wife says," Ethan chuckled. "But it is only because she is Irish, and not so fond of what the English have done to her country." A look of realization slowly crossed his face while he stared at Samuel. "What did you say your surname was?"

Samuel laughed nervously. "You caught me, Ethan. My

surname is O'Connell, same as your wife's. I'm your new brother-in-law."

Ethan laughed incredulously. "Why didn't you just say that you were Abigail's brother? We would have given you the job right away."

"That is the reason I did not say. I was not trying to be deceitful, only I wanted to prove myself as right for the job. It wouldn't be honorable if I got the job just for being related."

Ethan shook his head. "Well I'll be. I knew I liked you from the start, but could not figure why it seemed like I already knew you. Does Abigail know about this?"

"She's the one who wrote to me about the job," Samuel answered.

"Do you want to go into the house to see her? I imagine it has been a while," Ethan offered.

Samuel grinned. "Could I? I'd love to see Abby!"

Ethan led Samuel into the house to Abigail's door, but told him to wait in the hallway until after he talked to Abigail. "How are you feeling?" Ethan asked when he saw her.

Abigail managed a smile. "I am doing better, but I am still very sad for us and for the girls, of course."

Ethan nodded in response. "Have you talked to William about taking the ride to Philadelphia?"

Abigail frowned in disappointment. "I saw him earlier today, but he said it would be best to wait at least a few more days." Abigail paused, then casually questioned, "How is the new groundskeeper working out?"

Ethan walked over to the window so she could not see the mischievous smile crossing his lips. "Who, Samuel? He is just terrible! The kid wouldn't know a fence post from a hole in the ground." Ethan turned to see Abigail's reaction. She looked surprised then furrowed her brow.

"That is a shame. I hoped he would work out," she said.

Ethan walked toward the bed and sat down in front of her. "And why would you hope that?"

She gave him a wide-eyed look and stammered. "Oh—well I—I just hoped that we could be free to move to the manor house. Now it will take even longer to find a new groundskeeper. But perhaps you made Samuel nervous and that is why he did not keep up."

Ethan could no longer keep a straight face and burst out laughing.

"What is so funny?" Abigail demanded.

"I know that he is your brother, Abigail. I was just teasing you."

She gasped indignantly. "How could you be such a beast to me?" Abigail threw a pillow at him, but it only made Ethan laugh harder.

"That's what you get for keeping secrets from me," he finally answered.

"But Sam insisted that he earn the job on his own merit. I was sworn to secrecy!" she cried defensively.

Ethan smiled at her and stroked her cheek. "Do you want to see him? He is just out in the hallway."

Abigail's face lit up in delight. "Yes! Show him in, please!"

Samuel walked in when Ethan opened the door. "I got the job, Abby," he grinned, walking over to hug her.

"I'm so proud of you!" she cried. Then she turned to Ethan. "I tried to talk him into moving into the manor house with us, but he says he would rather work here."

"That's right," Samuel agreed. "I aim to buy a property

for myself and build a house on it with my own two hands. It is good to see you again, Abby. But for now, I gotta get back to work."

After Samuel left the room, Abigail smiled at Ethan. "Thank you for bringing him up here. It feels good to smile and laugh again, but I can't help but feel guilty for having joy in the midst of such sadness."

"I expect we'll have times of sadness for the rest of our lives. We should not miss the chance to feel the moments of joy that might come our way," Ethan told her. "It is what makes us alive."

"I suppose you are right," she agreed. "I love you."

Ethan leaned toward her and kissed her softly. "I made something for you," he whispered. He reached into his pocket and retrieved a small object, placing it into Abigail's hand before he left the room. "I love you too, Abigail."

She tearfully admired the tiny wood carving of a rocking horse, and treasured the loving hands that made it. At the bottom of one of the rockers were the words carved, *In Memory of Our Child, 1915.*

Chapter 14

Fiona met with Bridget and Jane in the servants' quarters. "We expect to hear that Miss Abigail will be moving to Philadelphia soon, and she will have Bridget as her personal maid. Jane, you will be attending the girls after Bridget leaves. I would like you to begin training with Bridget right away so you are prepared for your new duties."

"Yes, Ma'am," Jane said obediently.

Nora was hiding around the corner while Fiona spoke to the other maids. She strutted toward them and looked the maids up and down. "What is this? A meeting with the maids? Why wasn't I included?"

"I was just telling Jane that she will be attending the girls after Bridget leaves us. I have put out inquiries for a new housemaid and hope to fill the position by the end of the week," Fiona explained.

Nora responded angrily. "You can't be serious! Jane has worked here just as long as I have, and I'm her superior!"

"It was at Miss Clara's request that Jane be her new maid," Fiona responded. "Now, let's get back to work."

"I don't believe this," Nora muttered, turning for the

servants' stairs. She stormed up to Clara's bedroom and found her lying on the bed. "Miss Clara, I must speak with you."

Clara held her hand to her forehead as if in pain. "Can it wait, Nora? I am tired and have a headache."

"It is urgent—in fact it is something that has waited too long to be said. I cannot have it weighing on my conscience any longer. You see, I have caught a member of the staff stealing from you."

Clara groaned and sat up on the bed, rubbing her temples with her fingertips. "Stealing? Who do you mean?"

"It is Fiona, Miss. She has been forcing myself and Mrs. Malone to distribute food for Mr. Valenti from your very own kitchens. Fiona admits that she has been doing so without your permission. I think it is because she fancies Mr. Valenti, but certainly you must see how her behavior is not suitable for a housekeeper…"

"I already know about her taking food to Phillip. But I find it in very poor taste that you have come to me at a time like this to complain about such things. It is not your place to decide whether Fiona is suitable, and if I find that you are causing trouble downstairs, I will have her find a maid to replace you immediately. I know what it is like to serve in this house, and I have no patience for maids who stir up strife. I wish to be left in peace now." Clara lay back down on the bed and Nora scurried out of the room in a panic. Fiona watched her leave the room from the upstairs hallway.

"What were you doing in there?" Fiona demanded. "I hope you were not bothering Miss Clara in her time of grief."

Nora hung her head. "I'm sorry, Fiona. I won't cause trouble again. My mother has been ill for some time, and I desperately need this job. Please, if you have any compassion in your heart, don't send me away."

Fiona looked at her carefully. "I will not dismiss you if you behave yourself. Now go to the kitchen and see if Mrs. Malone requires your help with dinner."

Nora nodded respectfully. "Yes, Ma'am."

Ethan was startled by a knock at the door of the stable apartment. "Mary," he greeted her in surprise. "Is Abigail asking for me?"

"No, I just wanted to come talk, if it is alright," she said gently. "You see, I have done something dreadful."

"I can't believe that," Ethan replied.

"I told William that I never wanted to see him again," Mary confessed.

Ethan was taken aback. "Why would you do that?"

Mary sighed. "It was over something that does not seem so significant now. What I want to know is, do you think he would still want me, after the way I have spoken to him?"

"Then you did not mean what you said to him," Ethan said in a statement rather than a question.

"I meant it at the time, but now I am afraid that I have ruined things between us," she explained.

Ethan put his hand on her shoulder. "You must talk to him, Mary. He loves you dearly and I'm certain he would do anything for you."

Mary felt butterflies in her stomach. "Thank you for saying so. I know that I must talk to him, but I do not know how I will find the courage to do so. What if he does not want me back? Or maybe he will tell me all of the things that are wrong with me."

Ethan managed a smile. "Do you want to have a ride

over the fields? Abigail and I will be leaving soon, and there are not many more days that we can ride together like we used to."

Mary's face relaxed. "Yes, I would like that very much. Thank you." Ethan hugged her tightly for several moments, while neither of them said a word. Then they rode over the fields until the evening, feeling the the return of strength that both of them thought they had lost.

After the ride, Mary went into the house to check on Clara. She was staring blankly out the window of her bedroom, but managed a smile when Mary walked in. "How was your ride?" Clara asked her.

"It was much needed," replied Mary. "How are you feeling?"

Clara looked nostalgic. "I was just remembering when Nellie invited me to be her companion on the voyage. I wanted to go, desperately. But when I told Mother, she warned me not to go. That was the same night the stable caught fire, and Mother pleaded with me to stay at the house. She said that the fire was an omen. Can you imagine if I would have gone? Even if I had lived to see Britain, I would never have seen Mother again. It was as if she knew. She probably saved my life."

Mary smiled and sat next to Clara in front of the window. "Your mother was a great lady. Did you know that she saved me too? If not for her, I might be in a hospital for lunatic people right now."

Clara looked confused. "How could that ever happen?"

"Your mother found out that Mrs. Davenport was conspiring with Dr. Jones to lock me away. It was so she could control my inheritance," Mary explained. "But your mother stole the document from her and warned me just in time so that I could set things right with the trustee."

"Mary, how dreadful! I had no idea that Mrs. Davenport had done such a thing. I am sorry I ever suggested that you should listen to that woman. I still feel terrible for going to her about the estate."

"It is all forgiven now," Mary assured her.

Clara began to giggle. "I cannot imagine Mother stealing anything! She was always so proper."

Mary nodded. "The house will never be the same without her. Even the servants have been terribly grieved these last days. It was your mother who made the house what it is today."

"We must do all that we can to keep it great, Mary. Will you help me?"

"I will do anything you ask," Mary answered. "Only I should tell you that I am about to leave to see William again."

Clara's face lit up. "Good for you, Mary! I hoped that you would change your mind about calling off the engagement."

Mary nodded. "If he will agree to have me back, I will ask for a later wedding date so that I can be here with you and help with the house."

"No, you must be married on schedule," Clara insisted. "The flowers and church have already been arranged. I think it would do us all good to have a cheerful event to look forward to. I am certain that Mother would agree with me on this."

Mary smiled and kissed her cheek. "I believe you are right. Thank you, Clara. You and Abigail have become the dearest sisters I could have wished for."

Mary rehearsed what she was going to say to William

on the drive to the clinic. When she stepped in the door, she instantly recognized the woman who stood in the waiting area. "Good evening, I'm Nurse Anderson," the woman said chattily. "We are just closing up, but of course if there's an emergency, the doctor will see you—unless it can wait for tomorrow—Dr. Hamilton is still with a patient. Just tell me what seems to be the problem." Nurse Anderson was the woman that Abigail was afraid to speak to the day she and Mary went to town. Mary was beginning to see why Abigail wanted to get away.

"I will just wait here for Dr. Hamilton," Mary said, pointing to the chair by the desk.

"Then it is an emergency? You can tell me, whatever it is. Oh dear! Are you pregnant? Has your man left you?" the woman asked with wide eyes.

"What? No!" Mary cried aghast. "I only wish to speak to Dr. Hamilton."

"I see..." Nurse Anderson trailed off. "Let's get you to an exam table."

"No, it is really not necessary—" Mary was interrupted by Nurse Anderson taking her hand and leading her to a hospital bed behind a curtain.

"Now you just wait here. Dr. Hamilton will be with you in a jiffy." Nurse Anderson then pulled the curtain closed and walked away, much to Mary's relief.

Mary sat down on the bed, trying to recall the words she wanted to say to William. But when he pulled back the curtain, Mary just stared at him and could not remember what any of them were. William was also speechless as soon as he saw her there. He took a deep breath before approaching her. "Are you—feeling ill?"

Mary shook her head. "Nurse Anderson did not understand that I had only come to talk to you."

"I see. Nurse Anderson can be—overzealous," William said quietly.

Mary held back tears while she looked into his eyes. "I'm desperately sorry for what I said. I was wrong for expecting you to do any differently than you did."

William sighed in relief and sat on the bed next to her. "Does this mean you will still marry me?" he asked.

"I want to very much," Mary answered tearfully. "Only I did not know if you still wanted me after what I said."

"Of course I want you," William replied. "I only need to know that you understand what my job requires, and that I cannot tell you everything. It might mean some difficult times for both of us to not be able to speak of it."

Mary nodded. "Abigail told me—that she has been seeing you. And I understand now."

"I'm sorry, Mary," he said, reaching out to touch her hair.

"I don't know if you are allowed to tell me the answer, but I wondered if I offered my car for Abigail to take to Philadelphia…would she be able to make the journey then? She is anxious to move to the manor house as soon as possible."

William smiled. "It is good of you to offer, Mary. The poor girl has been through a great deal this year. First the poisoning, then the typhoid fever…now this. It has made her body weak and she should not be jostled around in a carriage for hours on end. I want her to have the strength she will need to live a long life. You may tell Abigail that I approve of a car ride to Philadelphia as soon as she wishes."

"She will be glad to hear it. Um…William," she said

slowly. "I asked the maids to set an extra place at dinner tonight. In case you are able to attend."

"I can't wait," he whispered as he leaned into her. "For the many things we will do together."

Nurse Anderson gasped when she pulled open the curtain and observed William holding and kissing Mary on the bed. "Doctor Hamilton!" she exclaimed.

William cleared his throat. "Forgive me, Nurse Anderson. I have not had a chance to properly introduce my fiance, Mary Davenport."

Nurse Anderson's expression changed to wonder. "Land Sake's! I had no idea you were engaged! Is it because she's pregnant? Because I won't tell a soul if that is the case."

William looked at Mary in confusion. Mary shook her head with a slight roll of her eyes, indicating that Nurse Anderson was mistaken. William answered quickly. "There is no baby on the way, but we are getting married just the same. We leave for the honeymoon in a few weeks." William squeezed Mary's hand.

"Very well, Doctor. Don't you worry about a thing. I will take excellent care of the patients while you are away," Nurse Anderson promised.

William stifled a laugh. "I am certain you will."

Later at Davenport House, Abigail was delighted when Mary offered the car for her to ride to Philadelphia. "It is a wonderful solution, Mary," she said. "And I am so pleased that you and William are alright now."

Mary blushed. "I am grateful that you told me I was in the wrong about breaking with him, and I am grateful that dear Mrs. Price wrote me this letter. Otherwise, I fear I might have made the biggest mistake of my life." She handed the letter to Abigail to read.

Miss Mary,

If you are reading this letter, it is because I am no longer with you. I am thankful for the kindness that you have always shown to Clara and me, and I wish you joy on your marriage to a great man. Please do not wear black for me. You have been wearing black for too long, and it is my final wish that you no longer be in mourning. You should begin your happy life with Dr. Hamilton, the same as you would have, if I had lived to see the day.

With Love,
Dorothy Price

Abigail smiled endearingly as she read the letter. "Has Clara seen this yet?" she asked.

Mary shook her head. "I am going to check on her now and show it to her."

"I am right here, Mary," Clara spoke from the doorway. "I wanted to ask if you and Abigail could join me for tea in the sitting room, just as we used to do."

"It is a wonderful idea," Abigail smiled. The three girls went to their usual places in the upstairs sitting room, which now emanated a feeling of warmth and tranquility. Abigail turned gently to Clara. "May I ask you something? I know that your dear mother has passed on, but do you have a feeling as if she has been here with us all this while?"

Clara looked thoughtful, then slowly smiled. "I feel as though she will burst through the door at any moment to remind me to get back to my studies. It is difficult to believe that she will never do so again."

"I think that she will always be with us in this house," Mary said. "Even the way the furniture is arranged in this room was directed by Mrs. Price. The house holds her essence in every room and in the placement of every object. It is almost as if she was the house itself." Mary blushed. "Sorry, I am rambling now and probably not making sense."

"It makes perfect sense, Mary," Clara said. "I will think on it when Abigail has moved to Philadelphia and you are away on honeymoon. It well help me not to feel alone in the house." The girls remained in the upstairs sitting room for the rest of the evening, reminiscing about dear Mrs. Price, and pondering how different life would soon be at Davenport House.

The day of the wedding arrived. The house was in a bustle as the servants and ladies prepared to attend the ceremony. Abigail stepped out of Mary's room to speak to Ethan, who was waiting in the hallway. "She is ready for you," Abigail grinned.

Ethan walked in and felt his breath catch in his throat when he saw Mary, looking radiant in her mother's wedding dress, her face shining with joy. "What do you think?" she asked.

Ethan tried to find the words. "I think you are beautiful," he said, his voice cracking. "Most times I cannot remember what our mother looked like because I was so young. But when I walked in the door just now, and you smiled at me—it's as if I am seeing her. I remember again."

Mary put her arms around her brother. "It is the most wonderful thing you could have said to me on my wedding day."

"You will have a swell honeymoon," Ethan remarked. "I hope to take Abigail to Niagara Falls someday."

"I promise to describe the falls in detail when we return," Mary stated. "We are so excited!"

Ethan could not help but stand there, grinning at Mary, feeling the happiness that filled the room. Then he realized the time was getting late. "Let's get you to the church before William gets worried."

Colorful rays of sunlight flowed in through the stained glass windows of the small church. Abigail seated herself on the pew next to Phillip Valenti and his family. "Why aren't you up there?" Phillip whispered, nodding toward the front of the church.

Abigail blushed. "Mary knows how nervous I get if I think that everyone is looking at me."

"I see," Phillip smiled.

The ceremony began and Clara walked down the aisle wearing a sunny yellow dress and holding a colorful bouquet of flowers. Ethan and Mary proceeded arm-in arm down the aisle after Clara. The wedding guests rose from their seats and William could hardly see Mary until she had reached the steps in front of the minister. She was soon standing in front of him with Ethan by her side.

"Who gives this woman to this man?" the minister began.

"I do," Ethan responded. He joined Mary's hand with William's and walked down the steps to sit next to his wife.

Abigail was soon sniffling as the ceremony continued. Ethan handed her the handkerchief from his breast pocket. "Are you alright?" he whispered.

Abigail nodded. "It is just—is there anything in the world more beautiful than a wedding like this?"

Ethan looked into her eyes and gently brushed the tears from her face. "Yes," he answered. "Knowing that you will someday be the mother to my children is more beautiful than anything I can imagine."

William smiled eagerly into Mary's eyes as he slid a gold wedding band onto her finger. He gently squeezed her hand and Mary smiled back at him while they waited for the minister to conclude the ceremony. Mary could not help but admire the wedding band, for she felt instantly comforted when William placed it there, and secure in the knowledge that it would stay on her hand from that day forward. At last, to the delight of everyone in the little church of Yorktown, the minister announced with great joy: "By the power vested in me by God and the Great State of Pennsylvania, I now pronounce that Dr. William Hamilton and Mary Lorraine Hamilton are man and wife!"

Chapter 15

Whitmore House, St. John's Wood, London

"Captain Perry is here to see you, Your Ladyship," Julia announced to Lucy Whitmore.

Lucy suddenly felt her knees go weak, but she tried to remain calm enough to reply. "Tell him I will be down in a moment, Julia." She smoothed her dress and looked at her reflection in the vanity mirror. Lucy sighed in disappointment and reached up for her hair that was pulled tightly into a bun. She began loosening several strands until realizing that she had gone too far and her hair became a mess. She removed the pins that held the bun in place and let all of her hair fall down, cascading like waterfalls over her shoulders. For a moment, her reflection almost looked like it had when she was only a young woman. She smiled slightly and decided to leave her hair down while she met with Frederick, no matter what Julia might say or think of it. She calmly walked down the stairs to the parlor.

"Good evening, Lucy," Frederick greeted, unable to keep from staring at her.

"Good evening," she replied. "I received your post about your having to leave for service in the Navy. I was not sure if I would see you again."

"I have just returned to London today," he answered. "The whole of the Royal Navy is perplexed as to why the Americans have not yet joined the war effort. It is sure to be only a matter of time before they come to our aid." Frederick sighed. "I am sorry that you and I could not finish our conversation that day."

Lucy nodded. "I am sorry too."

"How was your niece's wedding?" he asked.

Lucy smiled sentimentally. "Gretna Green is just as people say it is. We stopped at the first smithy on the way into Scotland, and Nellie and Henry were married there near an anvil. It did not rain, at least."

Frederick laughed. "I am happy for them and wish them well. I hope I am not interrupting your plans by stopping by. You look as if you are ready to leave for somewhere."

"I have been invited to dine at Caswell Castle," Lucy answered. "The Marquess cannot keep the castle for much longer, and we are trying to make the most of it while it is still in the family's possession."

"I see," Frederick replied. "Then I will leave you to your dinner plans."

"Wait," Lucy said. "Please do not leave yet. Why don't you come with me and dine at the castle?"

Frederick chuckled. "But it would be awkward to be the uninvited guest."

Lucy thought for a moment, then walked over to the telephone. She was soon connected and speaking with

Nellie. "Captain Perry has just returned from his Naval service," Lucy said into the telephone.

Frederick could hear Nellie shouting excitedly on the other end. "Oh! You must bring him with you! Henry will be delighted to see Captain Perry!"

"Very well, Nellie," Lucy smiled. "There are also two telegrams that were delivered here for you today. I will bring them with me tonight."

"Oh, I can't wait! Come quickly, Aunt!" Nellie shrieked.

Lucy returned the telephone to its cradle and turned to Frederick. "It seems you have been invited to dine at the castle after all."

"In that case, I would not wish to disappoint," he said, stifling a smile. "But may I speak to you for a moment before we leave? There is something I have wanted to say."

Lucy tried to ignore the sound of her heart pounding in her ears. She could not speak, but only nodded for him to continue.

"The letter that you wrote me…I'm terribly sorry you went through that, Lucy. I had no idea your parents locked you away. How dreadful it must have been."

Lucy held back tears as she remembered it. "And it must have been dreadful for you to wait in the rain and to think that I had changed my mind, when in truth I never would have done so."

Frederick appeared hopeful after her reply. "Lucy, there were two things you wrote in your letter, and I want to set them right before another moment passes. The first that I want to say is, I could never hate you. The second is, that I could never forget you."

Lucy did not realize she was holding her breath while Frederick spoke. She began to gasp for air and soon felt his arms around her, holding her with with love that had waited for decades. "Lucy," he said, beginning to stroke her hair. "Tell me if you think we could try again. It is true what your niece has said about life being short. I want to be with you for however many years we have left."

"And I want to be with you," she whispered.

Frederick breathed in relief. "Then there is no reason that we should not be married just as soon as we have finished this dinner tonight. Let's not wait for marriage banns."

Lucy pulled away from him and laughed. "Truly? You wish to drive to Scotland directly after dinner?"

"And we will stop at the first smithy we find. I don't want to waste another minute," Frederick said, laughing with joy. He held her hands in his and they smiled at each other for a long while.

"We mustn't keep my niece waiting," Lucy finally said. "Let us leave for dinner. Afterward, we will drive to Scotland."

Frederick and Lucy arrived at the castle and met Nellie and Henry in the grand entryway. "Aunt Lucy!" cried Nellie, throwing her arms around her aunt. "Do you have the telegrams? I am anxious to hear news from home. Are they from my mother?"

"One is from Davenport House," Lucy said, retrieving the envelopes from her handbag. "The other—is from your father."

Nellie's expression became serious. "Oh, I see. I will open the one from Mary first. It is bound to be cheerful news." She opened the telegram with enthusiasm and began to read. "Goodness! She has married Dr. Hamilton! And they honeymooned in Niagara Falls! Oh Henry, I hope that we may see the falls if we ever return to America. Mary says they are breathtaking!"

"Of course we will see the falls, if you wish," Henry replied with a smile. He knew it was no use talking Nellie out of her ideas anyway. "Are you going to tell your friend Mary about our news?" he asked, placing his hand over her belly. Lucy looked at Nellie expectantly after Henry did so.

"Not until we know the name for sure. There is nothing more vulgar than the announcement of a baby when the name is not even mentioned!" Everyone laughed at Nellie's remark.

"I suppose I must read this telegram from Father now," Nellie said reluctantly. She opened the envelope and began to read. Her face turned pink as she glanced over the words many times over to ensure that she had read them correctly.

NELLIE CASWELL
WHITMORE HOUSE, ST JOHNS WOOD, LONDON

YOUR NEW BROTHER IS CALLED GEORGE WHITMORE III STOP WE LOVE YOU AND WISH YOU WELL WITH LORD HENRY STOP YOUR SECURITY IS ASSURED FOR I HAVE KEPT YOU AS HEIRESS TO HALF THE FORTUNE STOP

JEREMIAH WHITMORE

When Nellie was silent, Henry looked at her compassionately and said, "Perhaps we should have waited until after dinner for you to read it."

"No, it is alright," she said, her voice catching with emotion. "My father writes to say that he loves me—and that I have a new brother."

Henry smiled at her. "I am glad for you, Nellie. Let us go up to dinner to celebrate." He held Nellie's hand as they ascended the staircase, and noticed that she was smiling blissfully. "Was there something else?" he asked her.

Nellie sighed in contentment as she showed him the telegram. "I have just remembered the words you said to me that day on the lifeboat, when our ship was sinking and it looked as if all hope was lost: we are safe, and everything will be alright."

...excerpt from Book 5...

DAVENPORT HOUSE

For the Cause

MARIE SILK

"Advance! Advance!" the lieutenant-general was shouting. The deafening roar of artillery shells coupled with the cries of men nearly drowned out the order altogether. Phillip Valenti stared in anguish at the barricade before him, knowing it was all that was left between their regiment and the enemy. Just as Phillip took the first step forward, he felt a hand forcibly grab his shoulder.

"Valenti!" Ethan yelled into his ear, even though their faces were only inches apart. Phillip turned his head to lock eyes with him while Ethan continued. "If anything happens to me, swear that you will care for Abigail and Mary!"

"I swear!" Phillip cried back. "And if anything happens to me, look after my family! Be a father to my children!"

"I swear!" shouted Ethan. They soberly shook hands before charging past the safety of the barricade, rapidly approaching the peril at the front line. Bullets were flying and men were dropping to the ground, causing the realization to those left standing—that it would take a miracle for any of the them to return home alive.

...coming Fall of 2016...

About the Author

Marie Silk has enjoyed writing stories and plays since child-hood. She lives with her family in the United States and frequently travels the globe to learn more about the world and the people in it. Marie is inspired by history and the feats of humanity from ancient civilization to present day. She is the author of the Davenport House family saga.

Emails may be sent to mariesilkpublishing@gmail.com.